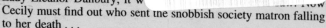
Room

The view from the Pennyfo
Lady Eleanor Danbury, it w
Cecily must find out who sent the snobbish society matron falling
to her death . . .

Do Not Disturb

Mr. Bickley answered the door knocker and ended up dead.
Cecily must capture the culprit—before murder darkens another doorstep . . .

Service for Two

Dr. McDuff's funeral became a fiasco when the mourners
found a stranger's body in the casket. Now Cecily must close
the case—for at the Pennyfoot, murder is a most unwelcome
guest . . .

Eat, Drink, and Be Buried

April showers bring May flowers—when one of the guests is
found strangled with a maypole ribbon. Soon the May Day
celebration turns into a hotel investigation—and Cecily fears
it's a merry month . . . for murder.

Check-Out Time

Life at the Pennyfoot hangs in the balance one sweltering summer when a distinguished guest plunges to his death from his
top-floor balcony. Was it the heat . . . or cold-blooded murder?

Grounds for Murder

The Pennyfoot's staff was put on edge when a young gypsy
was hacked to death in the woods near Badgers End. And now
it's up to Cecily to find out who at the Pennyfoot has a deadly
axe to grind . . .

Pay the Piper

The Pennyfoot's bagpipe contest ended on a sour note when
one of the pipers was murdered. Cecily must catch the killer—
before another piper pays for his visit with his life . . .

Chivalry is Dead

The jousting competition had everyone excited, until someone
began early by practicing on—and murdering—Cecily's footman. Now she must discover who threw the lethal lance . . .

MORE MYSTERIES FROM THE
BERKLEY PUBLISHING GROUP ...

DEATH WITH RESERVATIONS

Kate Kingsbury

BERKLEY PRIME CRIME, NEW YORK

DEATH WITH RESERVATIONS

A Berkley Prime Crime Book / published by arrangement with the author

PRINTING HISTORY
Berkley Prime Crime edition / January 1998

The Putnam Berkley World Wide Web site address is
http://www.berkley.com

ISBN: 0-425-16144-7

Berkley Prime Crime Books are published
by The Berkley Publishing Group, a member of Penguin Putnam Inc.,
200 Madison Avenue, New York, NY 10016.
The name BERKLEY PRIME CRIME and the BERKLEY PRIME CRIME
design are trademarks belonging to Berkley Publishing Corporation.

PRINTED IN THE UNITED STATES OF AMERICA

10 9 8 7 6 5 4 3 2 1

CHAPTER

1

The warm September sun bathed the Esplanade as Madeline Pengrath wafted alongside the railings that separated the sands from the street. The light breeze from the ocean lifted her dark hair, and the long strands floated behind her like smoke from a bonfire.

Dressed in pale cream gauze, with the hem of her skirt drifting around her bare ankles, her ghostly figure appeared to skim above the ground as she crossed the street to the steps of the Pennyfoot Hotel.

More than one head turned to watch her progress, perhaps fascinated by her graceful, almost ethereal glide and the proud tilt of her head. Some who recognized her quickly looked away. It was dangerous to stare too long at a witch.

Unaware of the stir she caused, Madeline mounted the steps, her thoughts centered on the woman who had summoned her to the hotel.

Bella DelRay, so she'd been told, was something of a celebrity in London, though here in the sleepy village of Badgers End, it was doubtful if many had heard of her.

In the years preceding this year of 1909, the entertainment in the music halls had undergone a drastic change. Where once musicians produced soft, lilting music from the strings of their violins and sweet-voiced sopranos trilled romantic melodies, the stage now resounded with the harsh, often vulgar, always suggestive songs delivered by well-endowed, robust women and coarse, leering men.

Variety, that loud, bawdy, sensational production aimed at the lower classes, had all but obliterated its genteel predecessor. Bella DelRay, according to Madeline's research, was an enthusiastic exponent of the modern spectacle. Bella DelRay was, in fact, a Variety star.

Madeline reached the front door of the hotel and bestowed one of her rare smiles on Ned, the doorman, who held the door open for her to step inside.

Ned responded with a cheerful wink. "Morning, Mrs. Pengrath."

"Good morning, Ned. How's the back?"

Ned's grin grew even wider. "Marvelous. That stuff what you gave me really did the trick. I don't know what was in it, but I had the best sleep I've had in years. Haven't felt a twinge since."

Well pleased, Madeline nodded. "I told you it would work."

"What's in it, then?" Ned asked, his voice low as he closed the door.

She laughed. "Just a few herbs and wildflowers. Nothing too mysterious."

"Go on, I know it's more than that." He gave her an anxious look. "Gertie told me you cast spells with those potions of yours. You didn't put a spell on me, did you?"

Madeline tilted her head to one side. "Now what kind of spell would I want to cast on you?"

"I dunno." He shrugged. "Maybe make me do something I wouldn't normally do?"

She shook her head at him. "No one can make you do that, Ned. It all depends on what you believe. All I did was give you a salve to ease your back. There's no magic in it."

He looked relieved. "I knew that Gertie was teasing me. I just wanted to make sure, that's all. You know how people talk, and she's not the first one to tell me you're a—" He broke off, looking embarrassed.

"I let people think what they want." Madeline glanced around the lobby. There were several people at the desk, waiting for their room keys. A tall, heavyset young woman wearing a fashionable light gray suit and a large pink hat stood by the grandfather clock, peering anxiously at the face as the Westminster chimes struck a quarter past the hour.

"I'm looking for Miss Bella DelRay," Madeline murmured after Ned had greeted two more guests. "I have an appointment with her."

Ned looked surprised. "You do? She's right over there, by the clock. Bit of a smasher, don't you think?"

Madeline studied the woman. She'd expected someone a little more gaudy. "You're sure that's Miss DelRay?" she asked doubtfully.

Ned looked astounded. "Cor, where you been? Don't you recognize her? She's been in all the papers, she has. I thought everybody knew who she was."

It was on the tip of her tongue to inform Ned that she wouldn't be caught dead at a Variety concert, but she wisely refrained. "Thank you, Ned. Let me know if you have any more trouble with your back."

With Ned's profuse thanks ringing in her ears, Madeline made her way over to the worried-looking woman.

"Miss DelRay?" she murmured as she reached the woman's side.

Wide blue eyes became riveted on her face. "Yes, I am. Are you—?"

"Madeline Pengrath."

"Oh, thank goodness," Bella DelRay muttered. "I thought you weren't coming." She sent a hunted look around the lobby, then, grasping Madeline's arm, pulled her into the dark corner behind the clock. "Did you bring it?"

For answer, Madeline unfastened the white silk pouch fastened to her belt. "I apologize for being late," she said quietly. "I was a little low and had to mix some more."

The singer took the pouch from her and peeked inside. "You're sure this will work?"

"Absolutely, if you follow my directions." She took a folded piece of paper from her pocket and handed it over.

Bella took it, then removed a bank note from inside her glove. "Here, I think this is right. I—" She broke off with a loud gasp.

Looking up, Madeline saw the singer's gaze fixed on something behind her. The expression on her handsome face could only be described as sheer disbelief.

Glancing over her shoulder, Madeline saw an elegant couple cross the floor toward the desk. The man was white-haired, and the protruding mid-section beneath his waist-coat suggested a self-indulgence so typical of the aristocracy, in her opinion. The woman at his side was quite tall, her face almost hidden by the large brim of her hat as she stepped daintily across the carpet in high-heeled boots.

"I don't believe it," Bella muttered, her voice holding such vehemence that Madeline was quite startled.

She studied the couple for a moment or two and was about to turn back to the singer when she saw the gentle-man's glance flicker over to their corner. He gave a visible start of surprise, so much so that his companion tilted her chin up to follow his gaze. The woman's dark brown eyes skimmed over Madeline, and then beyond to where Bella stood.

Apparently disinterested in what she saw, she then turned

to her escort, who appeared to have recovered and was smiling fatuously at her.

Intrigued by this little byplay, Madeline turned back to Bella. The singer kept her eyes on the couple until they left the lobby, then she let out her breath on a relieved sigh. "That was close," she muttered.

"I take it you know the gentleman," Madeline said, pocketing the bank note.

"He's the reason I'm here," Bella said in a low, angry voice. "He must have followed me down here. He's the one who put me in this predicament. If it wasn't for him, I wouldn't be here now buying poison to get rid of the baby."

"It's only poison if you take too much," Madeline said mildly. "It's oil of tansy, milked from a wildflower. Taken in the proper dose, the worst it will do is make you nauseous."

"I'm that now," Bella said fiercely, "thanks to that pompous oaf. Worst thing I ever did was agree to spend an evening with him. He forced his attentions on me, and this is the result."

"I'd make him pay for the potion," Madeline said, wondering why the singer would want to associate with a man like that.

"I tried. He not only refused, he told me if I breathed a word to anyone he'd ruin my career on the stage." Bella grimaced. "He could do it, too. He knows a lot of important people. I'm not about to take that chance."

"Just be careful with the potion," Madeline said, glancing at the clock. "Remember, if you take too much, it could possibly kill you."

"I'll remember." Bella sent a dark look across the foyer to where the couple had disappeared. "I'm not about to give up my life because Lord Bertram Sittingdon couldn't control his ardor. I do wonder, though, what his wife would say if she knew."

"Well, if you value your career," Madeline said, "I would advise you not to mention it to her."

"Don't you worry. I won't." She gave Madeline a tight little smile. "Thank you, Miss Pengrath. I appreciate your help."

"I'm happy to have been of service, Miss DelRay. I hope everything works well for you." Taking her leave, Madeline left the singer standing there, still staring across the foyer as if she wished she could send Lord Bertram Sittingdon down a bottomless black pit, never to return.

Belowstairs, the subject of Bella DelRay caused some dissension in the kitchen. Ever since Samuel, the stable manager, had told the maids about the arrival of the celebrated singer, Doris, one of the newest members of the staff, had been floating around on a pink cloud of expectation.

She stood at the kitchen sink, her scrawny arms covered to the elbows in soapy bubbles, and swished dinner plates back and forth while she hummed a pretty tune in a soft, melodious voice. Her twin, Daisy, stood near the door, holding a plump, rosy-cheeked baby in each arm.

"Just because there's a singer in the hotel," Daisy declared, "doesn't mean she'll be able to get you on the stage, Doris. She probably won't even talk to you."

Doris stopped humming and looked over her shoulder at her sister. "I'll find a way to talk to her. This is my first big chance to talk to a real Variety star, and I'm not going to let anything stop me."

"You'll get into trouble if you make a nuisance of yourself," Daisy said, looking worried. She shifted the babies higher on her hips. One of them whimpered, and she dropped a kiss on top of the fragrant downy head.

Doris used one wet hand to hitch up the apron that always looked too big for her. "I'm not a nuisance. Singers should be glad when people want to talk to them. One day when I'm a big star too, I'll be glad to talk to anyone what wants to, so there."

A buxom young woman with untidy black hair tucked beneath her white cap appeared in the doorway. "What the bleeding heck are you two nattering about now?" Gertie demanded. "I thought you were going to take me babies for a bloody walk, Daisy."

"I am, Miss Brown," Daisy said hurriedly. "I was just on me way out."

"Well, let me give them a kiss before you go." Gertie smacked each baby on the cheek. " 'Bye, James. 'Bye Lilly. Behave yourselves now." She watched Daisy carry the twins out of the door, then turned back to Doris. "Haven't you got them bleeding dishes done yet? It'll soon be time to lay the tables for dinner at this rate."

"I'm going as fast as I can," Doris mumbled. She shoved a hank of light brown hair out of her eyes and left a streak of bubbles across her perspiring forehead. Dragging a plate from the water, she shook it to release the suds before standing it on the draining board. "Have you seen Bella DelRay?" she asked hopefully as Gertie stomped across the floor to the stove.

"Yeah, I took a tray up to her this morning. I didn't think she was bleeding nothing. To hear you talk, I thought she was really glamorous, like the pictures of those fancy women in the magazines."

"She *is* glamorous when she's on stage," Doris said, reaching for another plate. She had to stand on tiptoe to reach down into the sink. Ever since she'd turned fifteen she'd been hoping she'd grow a bit more. She used to be the same height as Daisy, but now her twin was getting taller than her.

It wasn't fair, Doris thought, slapping the plate down on the draining board. She was the one what wanted to be on the stage, and she needed to be taller to look glamorous. All Daisy cared about was taking care of Gertie Brown's twins. She didn't need to be tall for that.

The door opened, and a smiling young woman tripped into the kitchen, carrying a large tray of soiled silverware.

"This is the last of it, Doris," she said, dumping the tray with a loud clatter onto the scrubbed wooden table in the center of the kitchen.

"Thanks goodness," Doris muttered. "Some days it never seems to end."

Ignoring her, Ethel turned to Gertie. "I just saw the two suffragettes, Gertie," she said, her voice rising with excitement. "They were going out the French windows with tennis racquets in their hands. Perhaps if we get done in time we can catch them on the way back from the tennis courts and talk to them."

"What's a suffragette?" Doris asked, tilting the tray so that the silverware slid into the steaming water.

Gertie waited until the deafening clatter subsided. "Don't you read nothing, Doris? It's in the bloody newspaper every day about them women what bleeding chain themselves up to railings and set fire to the flipping posh men's clubs."

"Oh, them." Doris lifted a fork and studied it for a moment before dropping it back into the water. "I only read about the theater. I don't have time to read anything else."

"Well, I think they deserve medals for what they do," Ethel said stoutly. "Look at all they suffer just so us women can do what men do."

"I don't know as I'd want to do what men do," Doris said, but no one was listening to her. Gertie and Ethel were off again, talking to each other and ignoring her as usual.

"Anyhow," Gertie said with a smug note in her voice, "I already talked to them, didn't I."

Ethel gave a gasp. "No, go on! When did you talk to them, then?"

"Last night. I was taking a tray up to that blinking toff's room, Lord Sittingdon, and I met them flipping suffragettes on the stairs. I knew who they was 'cause I saw a picture of them last week in the paper." Gertie's voice dropped to a confidential murmur. "They've been in bleeding prison, they have."

"Gawd, how awful. What did they do?"

"They dug dirty great holes all over a golf course, that's what. Then they chained themselves to the flipping doors of the gentleman's club so as no one could get in or out."

Ethel giggled. "I expect that made them mad."

"It did. That's why they got sent to the bloody clink. When I saw them last night I asked them if they wanted anything, like I'm supposed to, and they said as how they'd like the bloody tray I was holding. I told them I was taking it to Lord Sittingdon's room, but I'd bring another one up for them if they wanted it. After that, they wouldn't stop talking."

Ethel's voice was hushed with awe. "What did they say, then?"

"They told me their names, didn't they, though I bleeding knew them already." Gertie uttered a loud sneeze, making Doris jump.

"Bless you," Ethel murmured.

"Anyway," Gertie said, wiping her nose on the back of her sleeve, "the tall one is Winnie Atkins, and the little one is Muriel Croft. I said as how I knew they'd been in prison, and they said they suffered terrible agony before the bobbies let them out again. They both look like bloody skeletons. I reckon they didn't have any bleeding food for weeks."

"I know, they really look ill." Ethel heaved a loud sigh. "I wonder if it's worth all that, just to get men to treat us proper."

" 'Course it is," Gertie said, banging a saucepan onto the stove. "Bleeding men can do what they like, but us women have to do what they tell us. We can't even choose who we want in the blinking government, like the men do. No wonder they make all the rules to suit the men. We have to bleeding put up with it."

"I know," Ethel muttered. "It isn't fair."

"Well, we ain't going to bloody put up with it much longer. We're just as good as men, and we weren't put on this flipping earth to be their bleeding slaves.''

"I'd be most 'appy if you would tell me what it is you are on ze earth for,'' an irritated voice with a decidedly French accent said from the doorway.

Doris almost dropped the plate she was wiping dry as Michel, the hotel's short-tempered chef, stalked into the kitchen.

"What eez all this chitter-chatter going on?'' the chef demanded. "Look at ze time. That is, if anyone here can tell ze time. Where are my eggs for the omelettes, I ask you? How do I make ze souffles if I do not have ze eggs?''

"I'll get them for you,'' Ethel choked out, and fled for the pantry.

"Sacre bleu!" Michel swept a hand across the stove, sending a saucepan crashing to the floor. Doris held her breath as he yelled, "This fire is not hot in the stove. Why is there not coal in the scuttle? I have to start cooking in twenty minutes, and ze fire is almost gone. Get me some coal, *tout de suite!"*

"Strewth,'' Gertie muttered. "Keep your bleeding hair on. Get the flipping coal, Doris, before he has a bloody fit and starts foaming at the bleeding mouth.''

"And you, Gertie,'' Michel roared. "You get me ze cognac from the larder, or it will be your mouth that is foaming from the soap I put into it.''

"Flipping heck,'' Gertie said indignantly, "what got you in a bleeding tizzy this morning?''

For answer, Michel sent another saucepan crashing to the floor.

Doris closed her eyes. Days like this made her wish with all her heart that she could escape to a world where all she had to do was stand on a stage and sing her heart out.

One day, she promised herself, she'd be up there, listening to the applause and taking her bows. Then there'd be no more Michel or his strange moods to worry about.

Humming a defiant tune inside her head, she grabbed hold of the coal scuttle and scurried out of the back door.

CHAPTER

2

Cecily Sinclair, the owner of the Pennyfoot Hotel, sat at the head of the long, Jacobean table in the library waiting with apprehension for her Entertainments Committee to arrive.

Ever since she and her late husband, James, had refurbished the stately manor and turned it into a hotel, it had been the Pennyfoot's tradition to hold a special event every week for the benefit of the guests.

Together with her two closest friends, Madeline Pengrath and Phoebe Carter-Holmes, Cecily organized the events, even though she was well aware that the majority of her well-heeled customers were more interested in the gaming rooms hidden away in the cellars, or the private boudoirs where a bored aristocrat could pleasantly while away the hours with forbidden fruit.

Cecily had more than the upcoming annual Harvest Ball

on her mind, however. She had an important announcement to make, and she was unsure of how her friends would react.

Phoebe was the first to arrive, as always. Trim and elegant in a pale mauve suit edged in black, she bustled into the library with the barest of taps on the door.

"Oh, my," she said with a gasp, tipping up her chin so that she could look at Cecily from under the enormous brim of her black hat. "I really thought I was going to be late today. Algie asked the members of my dance troupe to help him decorate the church for the Harvest Festival."

"Oh, dear," Cecily murmured.

"I can't imagine what he was thinking of. He should know better than anyone the trouble those girls can get into. He may be the vicar of this parish, but I do wish he would listen to his mother once in a while. I told him over and over again that those girls can't be trusted to dress their own hair, let alone decorate a church."

She sat down, dropping her parasol onto the floor while she fussily arranged the folds of her long skirt to allow her matching shoes to peek out from beneath the hem.

"What did they do this time?" Cecily asked, trying to visualize the finicky vicar in charge of the unruly, rebellious group of young women with whom Phoebe invariably had an ongoing battle.

Phoebe uttered a genteel groan. "Don't even ask, my dear. When I left, after restoring some semblance of order, the entire church was strewn with corn husks and squished fruit. Apparently Marion had infuriated some of the other girls, and the entire group resorted to flinging the decorations at each other. You can't imagine the mess."

Cecily could, but she was saved from commenting by the arrival of Madeline. The willowy woman sauntered into the room with a languid wave of her hand before dropping onto the nearest chair.

"It has turned unusually warm for September," she remarked, dabbing at her forehead with the back of her hand.

Phoebe tutted. "If you would simply wear a hat when you're out in the sun, Madeline, your skin wouldn't scorch to that unbecoming color."

Madeline cast a bored look at her. "And if I wore a hat as constantly as you do, Phoebe dear, I would not have this abundance of hair on my head."

Cecily winced, reminded of the rumors around the Pennyfoot that Phoebe was bald, which explained why she was never seen without one of her monstrous hats.

Phoebe sat up straight in her chair, her cheeks turning pink. "It is customary for a lady to wear a hat when she is outdoors," she said stiffly.

"It is also customary for a lady to refrain from making malicious comments," Madeline answered with a remarkable absence of inflection in her voice. "There are some among us, however, who pay scant attention to propriety."

"Have you decided on the flowers you will use to decorate the ballroom?" Cecily asked loudly. Once Phoebe and Madeline began their usual sparring, there was no telling where it would end. Cecily had learned from painful experience that the time to intervene was as early as possible.

"Oh, definitely chrysanthemums," Madeline said, abandoning her skirmish with Phoebe for her favorite subject. "Those huge yellow ones, I think. Dahlias, too, if I can get the right colors. There are plenty of bulrushes about this time of year, so I should be able to arrange a nice display."

Cecily smiled. "You always do, Madeline." Ignoring Phoebe's loud sniff, she turned to that lady. "What about the entertainment, Phoebe? Have you managed to arrange something for us?"

"Yes, I have." With a disdainful look at Madeline, Phoebe made a big display of smoothing the creases out of her elbow-length gloves. "As a matter of fact, I have found a quite exquisite little man who can imitate just about every bird call imaginable. Mr. Tootle's whistling is quite unique, and most enchanting."

"Whistling?" Cecily repeated faintly, while Madeline snickered. "Are you quite sure he can carry an evening's entertainment, Phoebe?"

"Oh, I'm sure he could." Phoebe nodded emphatically, sending little wisps from the massive black ostrich feather on her hat drifting to the floor. "He whistles tunes as well, you see. I have also arranged for a gentleman and wife dance team to perform, however, in order to give Mr. Tootle's lips a rest. All that puckering can be quite dehydrating, you know. It's very difficult to whistle when your lips are dry, so I understand."

"That explains why the crows make that dreadful noise in summer," Madeline said, giving Cecily an unladylike wink. "Lack of water."

Cecily gave her friend a quick frown. She wasn't in the mood for Madeline's teasing this morning.

Madeline must have sensed as much, as she leaned forward with an intent look in her dark eyes. "Is everything well with you, Cecily? You seem a little strained."

Now that the moment was at hand, Cecily wasn't quite sure how to present her news. "I do have something on my mind," she admitted, while Phoebe sat back with a slight sound that warned Cecily she was miffed.

"Well," Madeline said in her soft voice, "out with it. I can tell it's good news."

Cecily's gaze involuntarily strayed to the large space on the wall above the massive marble fireplace. Until recently, her late husband's portrait had hung there in silent splendor.

James Sinclair had cut a dashing figure in his military uniform, and had long gazed down on his widow as she conducted her business at the head of the library table.

Now the wall where it had once hung was empty, with only a faint shadow against the slightly faded wallpaper to remind her of its former presence.

Without turning around, Madeline said quietly, "James has gone, hasn't he, Cecily?"

Aware of her friend's strange powers, Cecily felt a chill

on her arms. She could have sworn that Madeline did not notice the absence of the portrait when she came in, and she had sat with her back to the wall since.

Phoebe uttered a sharp exclamation and turned her head to look at the wall. "Cecily! What happened to James's portrait? Did it fall? Oh, I do hope it isn't damaged. I know how much that portrait means to you."

"It didn't fall, Phoebe." Cecily cleared her throat and clasped her hands on the table in front of her. "I had Samuel take the portrait down last night."

"Take it down?" Phoebe gave her a bewildered stare. "I don't understand. Is there something wrong with it?"

Madeline's gaze sharpened. "Baxter," she said softly.

Cecily nodded. She might have known that Madeline would guess. "Baxter will be returning to the Pennyfoot this afternoon to resume his duties as manager."

Phoebe uttered a small exclamation of surprise. "My dear, how terribly nice for you. Though I really don't understand why you didn't tell us about this before. When was all this decided?"

Cecily shrugged, avoiding Madeline's shrewd gaze. "Last month, actually. As a matter of fact, Baxter is now my business partner. I didn't wish to say anything until everything was settled."

Madeline slowly nodded. "Only a business partner?" she murmured.

"Only a business partner, Madeline." Cecily hesitated, then couldn't resist adding, "For the time being, at least."

"Ah!" Madeline sat back, looking very pleased.

Phoebe scowled at her. "Really, Madeline, I don't know where you get these ridiculous notions. Of course it is a business arrangement. Cecily would never dream of consorting with her manager. I'm aghast that you should even consider such an unseemly idea."

Madeline raised her eyebrows but refrained from answering, much to Cecily's relief.

"Though I must say," Phoebe went on, "I am most

surprised to hear that Mr. Baxter has become a partner in the hotel. Do you really think that is wise, Cecily?"

"I think it is probably the best decision I have made in a good many years."

"I heartily agree," Madeline said, eyeing Phoebe with distaste. "Thank heavens some of us have enough sense to grasp at opportunity when presented. The trouble with you, Phoebe, is that your nose is so high in the air you fail to see what is directly under it. Baxter is a fine man and an excellent manager. He will make a commendable partner, I am quite sure. Instead of voicing your disapproval, you should be congratulating Cecily on her good fortune."

"Well, really!" Obviously put out, Phoebe magically produced a lace-edged handkerchief from her sleeve and began fanning her face. "I only meant that when it comes to matters of finance, one should be cautious of one's associates. It doesn't do to rush into these things, as I well know."

Madeline sighed. "Perhaps if you were a little less persnickety, Phoebe, you might possibly have better luck with the gentlemen. There is many a precious stone to be found among the pebbles if one is only willing to explore."

"Yes, well, we all know how well acquainted *you* are with the pebbles."

Deciding it was time to intervene, Cecily said hastily, "Phoebe, I truly appreciate your concerns about my welfare but I assure you I can trust Baxter implicitly. I'm the first to admit that I need help with the running of this hotel, and who better than the man who has been my right hand for so many years?"

Only slightly mollified, Phoebe tucked her handkerchief into her sleeve. "Well, if you're that certain."

"I'm that certain," Cecily said firmly. "When Baxter left the hotel to take a position in London, I realized how lost I was without him. He must have come to the same realization, as he suggested the partnership a month ago. I accepted without hesitation."

"Well," Phoebe said, getting to her feet, "I think I will take my leave. For some reason I feel quite melancholy this morning. I feel in need of a long walk in the sun. I am happy that you have someone to lean on again. I can imagine how much you miss James. I know how lonely I have been since dear Sedgely died."

"Well, Phoebe, I am always willing to share a cup of tea with you at Dolly's tea shop, should you need company."

Cecily looked at Madeline in surprise. Sometimes her friend could be most unpredictable.

Phoebe looked stunned by this gracious offer. "Well, Madeline . . . how very nice of you . . . I should be delighted, of course . . . thank you so much. . . ." Choking on the last word, she pressed her gloved hand to her mouth and fled from the room.

"That was very nice of you, Madeline," Cecily said warmly. "I know how much Phoebe irritates you at times. She needs your friendship. She doesn't have too many friends, I'm afraid."

Madeline shrugged. "Neither do I, if it comes to that. Phoebe and I understand each other. We could do worse, I suppose." She shook her head wistfully. "I must admit, Cecily, I rather envy you your Baxter."

Cecily laughed. "You envy me? Why on earth should you?"

"You can't fool me." Madeline wagged a slender finger at her. "You forget, my friend, that I see all and know all. Your partnership may well be a business one on the surface, but I'm willing to wager that the bond between you goes far deeper than that."

Unable to deny what was in her heart, Cecily smiled at the lovely woman seated opposite her. "Why, Madeline, you could have your pick of half the men in Badgers End, and you well know it."

"I doubt that," Madeline said dryly. "Not too many men want to marry a witch. The point is, I am simply not capable of loving a man. I have accepted that fact, but there are times when I wish it wasn't so.''

There didn't seem to be an answer to that. In any case, they were interrupted just then by a sharp tap on the door. Thinking that it might be Baxter arriving from London, Cecily's heart skipped a beat.

It was Doris, however, who answered her summons to enter. She bobbed a quick curtsey before saying in a breathless voice, ''I'm sorry to disturb you, mum, but Lady Katherine has asked for a doctor to be sent to her suite.''

Cecily looked at her maid in dismay. ''She is ill? Did she say what is wrong?''

''No, mum, it's not milady what's ill. It's her husband, Lord Sittingdon. Lady Katherine says he's in dreadful pain, throwing himself all over the bed, he is. Took ill in the night, I believe. He wouldn't have the doctor until now. Milady says he must be really, really ill, 'cause he doesn't have no time for doctors.''

''Oh, dear,'' Cecily murmured. ''Thank you, Doris. Have Samuel fetch Dr. Prestwick at once. I'll go up to the suite and see if there's anything I can do.''

''Yes, mum,'' Doris said, bobbing another curtsey.

She disappeared out of the door, and Cecily sighed. ''How dreadful to become ill while on holiday. I do hope he isn't too sickly to enjoy the rest of his stay.''

''If you want my opinion,'' Madeline said, ''he'd do well to go home as soon as possible.''

Cecily looked at her in surprise. ''Why do you say that?''

She listened with growing dismay as Madeline recounted the events in the foyer earlier.

''I don't usually divulge the confidences of my customers,'' Madeline said when she was finished, ''but in this case I felt I should warn you. There could be trouble, seeing that the fool brought his wife along, though I have to admit he managed to look suitably surprised to see Bella.''

She frowned, smoothing her long fingers along the line

of her forehead. "Not that it seemed to matter. Judging by Lady Katherine's lack of concern when she saw Bella, I don't think she even recognized the lady. Or if she did, she is certainly not aware of her husband's unfortunate association with the woman."

"Perhaps we have nothing to worry about, then," Cecily said hopefully.

"Perhaps." Madeline continued to frown. "I do wonder, though, why Lord Sittingdon brought his wife along if he expected to meet Bella at the hotel."

"That does seem more than a little imprudent," Cecily agreed.

"More than imprudent. I'd say it was utterly stupid." Madeline paused, and Cecily watched an expression cross her friend's face that she knew well and had often dreaded.

"In fact," Madeline said, her voice chillingly soft, "I have the distinct feeling that Lord Sittingdon will pay for that mistake in a way he couldn't possibly imagine."

CHAPTER

❀ 3 ❀

By midday the warm sun had driven most of the guests out into the spacious gardens of the Pennyfoot. Samuel had been dispatched to the station to meet Baxter on the afternoon train, and Cecily, with another hour or so to wait for his arrival, decided to take advantage of the pleasant weather.

She had spent a worrying few minutes with Lady Katherine, who was obviously gravely concerned about her husband's ill health. Unsettled by the woman's fear for her husband, Cecily had felt the need to escape the confines of the hotel for a few minutes.

More and more lately, she was finding it difficult to deal with the problems that seemed to arise constantly at the Pennyfoot. There had been a time when she had accepted it all as part of the business, but now each little incident seemed to weigh heavily on her shoulders.

Aware that her lack of fortitude was due almost entirely to Baxter's absence, she tried to shake off her despondency with the reminder that after today she would be able to share her worries with him once more.

Crossing the freshly cut grass, she lifted her head in appreciation. The sun's rays dazzled her, and she briefly closed her eyes as the heat bathed her face. Before long the winter gales would sweep in from the North Sea, cutting to the bone any foolhardy person who stood in their way. One had to enjoy the fleeting moments of a dying summer, and the rare warmth on the skin that was such a luxury on the southeast coast of England.

The distant *pock* of tennis racquets and the more solid *smack* of wooden mallets echoed across the freshly cut lawns. Cecily paused to watch a small group of guests enjoying a game of croquet.

One young lady attacked the hardwood ball with such gusto that she tripped over the flounced hem of her pale lemon frock. Clutching the wide brim of her daisy-trimmed hat with one hand, she dropped the mallet and snatched at the arm of her escort. The gentleman gallantly righted her as a chorus of lilting laughter floated on the balmy sea breeze.

Beyond them, Cecily spotted John Thimble, the Pennyfoot's reticent gardener, heading for the duck pond. Now would be a good time to talk to him, she decided. She wanted to remodel the roof garden.

James had designed the rooftop refuge shortly after buying the hotel. The tiny garden bore his stamp; the painted half barrels filled with rose bushes, the dainty trellises heavy with honeysuckle, and the border boxes crammed with marigolds and chrysanthemums.

She and James had spent many a pleasant hour gazing out to sea or across the green velvet of Putney Downs, enjoying a brief respite from the hectic demands of the hotel.

Now Cecily wanted a different look to the garden. Although she had no wish to erase the memory of her late husband entirely, neither did she care to have his ghost intrude upon her new life.

Madeline, as always, had seen through her attempt at subterfuge. While it was true that Baxter had offered to buy a partnership in the hotel, he had also made it clear that his intentions were more personal. After years of rigidly denying his feelings, he had admitted a fondness for her that could lead to a more intimate arrangement, given time.

As always, the thought of Baxter gave her spirits a boost. She was no longer alone. Not only did she have her manager back, she had the promise of something infinitely more precious.

It seemed that she witnessed everything through senses sharpened by the changes in her future. She heard the sea breeze rustle in the branches of the elms, and tiny sparrows chirp from the dense, carved topiaries. The heady fragrance of late-summer blossoms beckoned to her from the rose garden.

Sunlight sparkled on the white walls of the hotel, and in the distance, seagulls wheeled above the dark blue waters of the quiet bay. She had a lot to be thankful for, she told herself, and she should not let her worries depress her. In all likelihood, Lord Sittingdon would soon recover and enjoy the rest of his stay at the Pennyfoot.

Shaking off her sense of doom, she hurried over to the duck pond, where John Thimble crouched at the water's edge. He looked up as she approached, his look of apprehension fading when he saw her.

''Morning, mum,'' he mumbled, his fingers straying to the floppy brim of his Panama hat. He pulled it off and crumpled it in his hands as he climbed awkwardly to his feet.

Cecily gave him a warm smile. John had been with the hotel since James had first bought it. A man of few words, he made no secret of the fact that he vastly preferred plants to people. He avoided contact with the human race as much as possible, though he lavished as much care on the vege-tables and flowers as a doting mother with her children.

In spite of his white hair and bowed back, he maintained the impeccable grounds of the hotel as well as any stalwart youth, refusing help of any kind.

"The chrysanthemums are coming along very nicely, John," she remarked, admiring the dancing golden heads bordering the pond.

"Yes, mum. Can't say the same about the hydrangeas, though."

Cecily looked at him in surprise. "There's something wrong with them?"

The hydrangeas formed a border between the tennis courts and the woods at the back of the hotel grounds. The last time she'd looked at them they were in full bloom, and certainly appeared healthy enough.

"You could say that, mum. Been attacked, they have."

"Attacked?" Cecily frowned, picturing a plague of vo-racious beetles or perhaps a horde of jackdaws bent on mischief.

"Yes, mum. Little blighters have been hacking off the blossoms."

"Hacking off?" Her imagination painted lethal beaks on the jackdaws.

"Yes, mum. With a pair of blunt shears, by the looks of it."

The attackers were apparently human, Cecily realized. Her thoughts immediately flew to Colonel Fortescue, a rather unpredictable gentleman who was prone to sudden outbursts of quite irrational behavior, supposedly due to his harrowing exposure to gunfire during the Boer War.

The colonel was a regular guest at the Pennyfoot, and the staff had learned to accept his unsettling, though harm-less antics, doing their level best to see that his disruptions did not upset the other guests. Whenever anything was strangely amiss at the hotel, however, one usually investigated the colonel's possible involvement before anyone else.

"I reckon it's them louts from the village up to mischief," John said, mopping his brow with a large, gray handkerchief. "I chased them away from the tennis courts the other day. I dare say they're looking for revenge."

"Oh, dear. Have they done much damage?"

John shook his head. "Chopped the blossoms off, that's all. I was going to prune them meself, but I'd've done a better job of it than the mess they made of it."

"I hope they don't go after the roses," Cecily said, throwing a worried glance across the lawns to where the vine-covered arbors sheltered the rose garden. "I'm afraid those bushes wouldn't stand up to that kind of treatment."

"Don't you worry, mum, those hooligans wouldn't get near them roses without me seeing them." John tucked the handkerchief back into the pocket of his trousers. "Must have come out of the trees back there. I'll keep a watch out for them."

"You will be careful, John?" Cecily eyed his frail figure with misgiving. "I wouldn't want to see you harmed in any way in defense of a few flowers."

John looked as if he were trying to throw back his shoulders—a feat that for him would be physically impossible. "I won't let no one touch my gardens, mum. That be my duty to protect what's mine."

Cecily didn't think this was the time to point out that the hotel and the grounds it sat on actually belonged to her. John's philosophy was simple. He owned what he created. In that sense, every plant in the gardens belonged to him. She wasn't about to argue the point.

Besides, she hadn't told him why she had sought him out. "I would like the roof garden renovated, John," she said, surprised at the ease with which she'd given the order.

John, who rarely revealed any expression whatsoever, had astonishment stamped all over his weathered face. "The roof garden, mum?"

He'd sounded as if she'd asked him to tear down the Sistine Chapel. "The roof garden, John," she said firmly. She could understand his dismay. James Sinclair had designed the garden, and to John the refuge was sacred.

"I'll see to it, mum," John said, his face expressionless once more. "Though I may need some help. Them there rose barrels weigh a bit."

"Of course. Ask whoever you like." She glanced back at the hotel, wondering how much time she had left before Baxter arrived.

"Yes, mum. Just as soon as I find out who's messing with me flowers."

Leaving him to plan his strategy, she hurried back to the hotel. She wanted to make sure she looked her best when she met Baxter.

She had chosen a simple tea gown of taffeta silk in a fine rose and white stripe in which to greet him. The new style favored a higher waist with a little more room to breathe, which pleased Cecily no end.

No one was happier to see the end of tight-waisted corsets—in fact, she couldn't wait to see the advent in England of the newest French mode of abandoning the corset altogether, though it would be some time before that particular style reached beyond the fashion circles of London.

The new fashion was quite becoming, she decided. With less material than she was accustomed to in the skirt, the gown graced the hips, falling in elegant folds to the floor. Satisfied with the ensemble, she decided to go without a hat, and pinned a silk rose to the Gibson collar instead.

As she drew on her gloves, a light tap sounded on the door. Her heart fluttered, and she took a deep breath. No doubt Baxter had arrived.

She opened the door to find Doris bobbing a curtsey. "Mr. Baxter is downstairs, mum. Shall I ask him to wait in the drawing room?"

"No, Doris. I think I shall meet him in the library. Please ask Mrs. Chubb to send up a bottle of sherry."

"Yes, mum." Doris dipped her knees again and then disappeared.

Cecily waited a few minutes longer before leaving her suite. It wouldn't do to appear to be in too much of a hurry. She wished, however, that she'd waited a little longer when she saw Colonel Fortescue at the head of the stairs.

"I say, old bean," he bellowed as soon as he set eyes on her, "you're looking absolutely ravishing, what? 'Pon my soul, I swear you're getting younger by the day."

Cecily smiled. "Thank you, Colonel. I trust you are feeling well?"

"Couldn't be better, old girl." He slapped his protruding stomach with the flat of his hand. "Just on my way for a spot of gin before lunch. Gives one a raging appetite, you know."

"I'm sure it does," Cecily murmured. She began to descend the steps, with the colonel hot on her heels.

"I must say, there's some dashed interesting guests staying here this week," the colonel boomed behind her. "I met those two hussies from London last night. In the George and Dragon, they were, in the public bar, mind you, bold as brass, knocking back pints like blasted bricklayers."

Guessing that he was talking about the two members of the Women's Movement, Cecily smiled. "That must have caused quite a stir."

"Stir, madam? It damn near caused a riot." The colonel sounded breathless as he tried to keep up with Cecily. Upon reaching the bottom of the stairs, he leaned against the banister for a moment, panting for air.

"I'm sure neither Miss Atkins nor Miss Croft meant any harm," Cecily said, glancing down the hallway toward the library. Her own heart was racing, but more from the delightful anticipation of seeing Baxter again than the exertion.

"Oh, quite so, old bean." The colonel straightened, and twirled the waxed ends of his white mustache. "As a matter of fact, I rather fancy the tall one . . . what did you say her name was?''

"Miss Atkins," Cecily murmured. "I'm sorry, Colonel, but I have someone waiting for me in the library. If you will excuse me?''

"Yes," the colonel muttered. "Miss Atkins. Reminds me of those African natives in the tropics. All blasted neck and no chin. Except they wore bones through their noses. Can't imagine how they slept with those ruddy things, much less snuggled up to anyone. Why, I remember once . . .''

"Excuse me, Colonel, I'm really late for my appointment." Cecily fled down the hall, leaving the colonel cheerfully recounting his memories to thin air.

As she reached the library she paused to take a deep breath. Countless times over the past years she had met Baxter in the library. She couldn't imagine why she should feel this disconcerted about doing so now.

True, things had changed between them, but certainly for the better. Anxious now to reassure herself that she hadn't imagined their conversation the last time they'd met, she hurried into the library.

Baxter stood by the French windows, and he turned to face her as she uttered a breathless "Hello."

He didn't answer her right away, but stood looking at her so long she became self-conscious. He looked elegant and sophisticated in his dark gray lounge suit. A clear indication of the change in Baxter since he'd moved to London was the gleaming gold watch chain draped across the front of his waistcoat. The old Baxter would not have bothered with such frivolous embellishment.

She searched in her mind for something clever to say, but could think of nothing.

"As always, dear madam," he murmured, "you are a sight for sore eyes. How could I forget what a great pleasure it is to look at you?''

She was not yet used to this new familiarity between

them and she had trouble meeting his gaze. "It's good to see you, too, Baxter. I hope you're ready for the trials and tribulations of running a hotel once more?"

"Indeed I am. I'm most anxious to resume my duties. I've already instructed Samuel to deposit my baggage in my former room. I assume that meets with your approval?"

"Of course. I've sent for a bottle of sherry. I thought it would be nice to toast your return with a glass before lunch."

She seated herself on one of the Queen Anne armchairs by the fireplace and watched him settle himself on the matching one. He glanced up at the wall as he leaned back. "I see you took down the portrait of James," he said quietly.

"Yes, I felt it fitting, under the circumstances."

He looked back at her, his expression grave. "I wouldn't presume to ask that you give up your memories of your former husband. He was my friend, and I would like to keep his memory alive."

"I shan't forget him," Cecily said, glancing up at the bare patch on the wall. "But the time for mourning is past. I have ordered that the portrait be hung in the ballroom. It was always James's favorite room."

He nodded. "As you wish."

She shifted uncomfortably on the chair, aware of a tension between them. Natural, perhaps, until they adjusted to their new roles, but she found herself praying that it wouldn't be too long before they fell back into the former pattern that had served them for so long.

"I'm sorry to break this to you in your first moments back," she said, glancing up at the clock on the mantel, "but I'm rather concerned about one of our guests. Lord Sittingdon has taken ill. In fact, we are waiting for the doctor to arrive at any minute."

He leaned forward and patted her hand. "Don't worry yourself too much over it. I'm quite sure he will quickly recover. If I remember, the gentleman is quite robust."

She smiled. "Have I ever told you that you are an immense comfort to me?"

"Not in so many words. I've often hoped, however, that I have helped to allay some of your fears in the past."

"Dear Baxter, you will never know—" The sharp tap on the door interrupted her.

Baxter sprang to his feet and opened the door with his customary flourish. Gertie stomped in, carrying a tray upon which balanced a bottle of sherry, two petite sherry glasses, and a large plate bearing a variety of canapés.

"Cor blimey, Mr. Baxter," she said, stopping to admire him. "You don't half look posh. Looks like one of them bleeding toffs, don't he, mum?"

"He does, indeed," Cecily agreed, enjoying Baxter's look of acute discomfort.

Gertie dropped the tray onto a small tea cart and pulled it over to the fireplace. "There you are, mum. Shall I pour for you?"

"Thank you, Gertie, but I think I'll let Baxter take care of it."

"Yes, mum." Gertie straightened her cap, which immediately slipped sideways again. "Will that be all, then, mum?"

"Thank you, Gertie."

The housemaid dropped a clumsy bob, then headed for the door. Halfway there, she stopped and swung around. One strap of her apron fell off her shoulder, and she shoved it back up again. "I almost forgot, mum. Dr. Prestwick is here. He went straight up to see the gentleman what's sick."

"Thank you, Gertie. Please let me know when he has completed his examination of the patient."

"Yes, mum, I'll be sure and do that." Again she bobbed a curtsey, grinned at Baxter, then promptly disappeared through the door.

Baxter gave a visible shudder as the door closed behind her. "I see that young woman still hasn't learned any decent manners. She is entirely too familiar. She needs to learn a little respect.''

"I doubt very much if Gertie will change at this late date," Cecily said mildly. "One does get used to it."

"Well, all I have to say is that it is time we made some changes around here."

She looked at him in amusement. "Why, Baxter, you were always so resistant to changes. The mere mention that there might be room for improvement in the hotel brought an instant scowl to your face."

He looked a little put out. "I admit I might have been somewhat cautious with regard to some issues, but I am more than willing to accept the fact that without change there is no growth. Now that I have a financial interest in the Pennyfoot, I am anxious to do whatever is best for the business."

For an instant Cecily felt a pang of misgiving. She had drawn swords with him in the past over their differing opinions on what was best for the hotel.

She hoped with all her heart that she had not made a mistake in accepting Baxter's offer of a partnership. The most important thing in the world to her was not so much what was best for the Pennyfoot, but what was best for her and Baxter. It would be ironic, indeed, if the management of the Pennyfoot turned out to be their undoing.

CHAPTER

❧ 4 ❧

Cecily was about to answer Baxter when another sharp tap sounded on the door. Once more he leapt to his feet, as if by old habit, and swept the door open.

A tall man with a head of luxurious blond hair stood in the doorway. He wore a grave expression on his handsome face, which changed to one of surprise when he caught sight of Baxter. "I had no idea you were in town," he said in a tone that suggested the revelation was not in the least pleasurable.

"I didn't think to warn you of my arrival," Baxter murmured smoothly.

Cecily rose rather quickly to her feet. She knew only too well how much Baxter abhorred Kevin Prestwick's familiarity toward her. The fact that the doctor treated every woman he met in the same manner did little to appease Baxter's irritation.

"How nice to see you, Kevin," she said, darting a look of reproach at Baxter. "I trust our patient is comfortable?"

The doctor bowed low over her hand, his lips lingering just a second too long. When he straightened again, the expression in his eyes caused Cecily a flutter of apprehension.

"I'm afraid I have grave news for you, Cecily," he said quietly. "I have examined Lord Sittingdon, and it is my considered opinion that the gentleman is too ill to return home. In fact, I regret to have to tell you that I am deeply concerned about his condition."

A cold chill passed over Cecily's back. She exchanged a worried glance with Baxter, then said anxiously, "What exactly are you saying, Kevin?"

"I am saying that I fear Lord Sittingdon may not recover from his illness."

Cecily uttered a small gasp of dismay. "Whatever is the matter with him? Is he infectious?"

"I sincerely hope not." Dr. Prestwick glanced at Baxter. "I hesitate to say more at this point."

Out of the corner of her eye Cecily saw Baxter bristle. "Anything you have to say can be said in Baxter's presence," she said quickly.

The doctor shrugged. "Very well. But it's unpleasant news, I'm afraid. I am quite sure that Lord Sittingdon is suffering from food poisoning."

Over Cecily's shocked cry, Baxter muttered something unintelligible.

As if he hadn't heard them, Dr. Prestwick continued in the same flat tone. "After talking with his wife, who insists that her husband ate nothing outside of the hotel, it would seem as if the contaminated food originated in the kitchen of the Pennyfoot. I don't think I need explain the consequences if that is found to be the case."

He did not, indeed. Cecily knew quite well that as owners of the Pennyfoot, she and Baxter would be held directly responsible for Lord Sittingdon's condition. Not only that, once the situation became widely known, the loss of business would be disastrous. It could well mean the end of the hotel.

"Are you sure you're not mistaken?" Baxter demanded in a proprietary tone that raised Prestwick's eyebrows.

"I assure you, my diagnosis is correct," the doctor said in a huff, sparing Baxter the merest of glances. Turning his attention back to Cecily, he reached for her hand. "I'm so sorry, my dear," he murmured. "I know what a worry this must be for you."

Fortunately he had his back to Baxter and missed the expression of pure outrage on her new partner's face. Quickly Cecily withdrew her hand from the doctor's grasp. "For us all, Kevin. I should inform you at this time that Baxter has agreed to return to the Pennyfoot, not only as my manager, but also as my business partner. I regret that his new position should begin with this unfortunate incident."

Prestwick straightened his back, a frown of disbelief marring his handsome face. "I had no idea," he muttered. For a moment he looked deep into her eyes, then, apparently recovering his composure, he turned to Baxter and gave him a stiff bow. "My congratulations, sir. A shrewd investment, if I may say so."

Cecily had the uncomfortable feeling he wasn't entirely referring to the financial aspect of the deal. If Baxter had the same idea, he showed no sign of it. In fact, he must have decided he could afford to be gracious. Inclining his head, he murmured, "Thank you, Doctor. I quite agree."

Once more Prestwick looked at Cecily, and this time there was no mistaking the reproach in his eyes. "I wish you well, Cecily. I'm sure this new arrangement must bring you a greater sense of security. It can't be easy for a woman to manage a business alone."

Cecily smiled at that. "I never have been alone, Kevin. Baxter has always been a great help and comfort to me. By accepting him as my partner, I am merely putting our relationship on an official footing.''

She glanced over at Baxter, who was watching her with a wary expression. ''And may I add,'' she said softly, ''it is well past time.''

Baxter cleared his throat. ''Well, what shall we do about Lord Sittingdon, then?''

Prestwick appeared not to have heard him at first, then, as if gathering his thoughts, he gave a small shake of his head. ''I'm afraid there is little we can do except wait.'' He headed to the door, as if anxious to make his escape. ''I have given Lord Sittingdon some medication that I hope will counteract the poison. I have left word with Lady Katherine to send for me if there is a change in her husband's condition.''

He reached the door and paused, looking back at Cecily. ''If Lord Sittingdon dies, I shall have to report the cause, of course. For the time being, however, I shall say nothing.''

''Thank you, Kevin. I appreciate your understanding.'' Cecily watched the door close behind him, then turned to Baxter. ''I simply can't believe that something Lord Sittingdon ate in this hotel caused him to become so ill.''

''The idea is preposterous, of course. I'm quite sure Lord Sittingdon will recover. Prestwick always did jump to conclusions.''

For once Baxter's assurances failed to comfort her. ''What if he is right?''

''Dear madam, please sit down and finish your sherry. Nothing will be gained by worrying yourself to death. As Prestwick says, we shall have to wait and see what transpires.''

Obediently she sat, though she had lost the taste for sherry now. ''What shall we do if Lord Sittingdon dies?''

''We will do what we have always done. Send for the doctor and have the poor wretch taken away.''

''That isn't what I'm concerned about,'' Cecily said, a

feeling of panic beginning to stir inside her. "If what Kevin says is true, and it was something from the kitchen that poisoned Lord Sittingdon, we shall be held responsible."

"Then we'll deal with the problem when it arises."

She couldn't believe he was being so indifferent about what could be a major tragedy. "Baxter," she said urgently, "can't you see the ramifications of the situation? If food from the kitchen is the cause of Lord Sittingdon's illness, then the other guests are in danger of being poisoned as well. We could have even more deaths on our conscience."

This time she saw his worried frown before he smoothed it out. She had to admire his effort to hide his anxiety. He wasn't indifferent, after all, she realized. He was just doing everything he could not to alarm her. That frightened her most of all.

"You should've seen him," Gertie said, the wide blade of her knife slicing deftly through a head of cabbage and scattering the pieces across the scrubbed wood table. "All toffed up, 'e was, like that bloody high and mighty Lord Sittingdon. Only he looked better, if you ask me. More 'andsome, like."

Ethel stood at the sink, the half-scrubbed carrot she held poised in midair. "You think Mr. Baxter is handsome?"

"Well, not as 'andsome as my Ned, of course."

Ethel's blue eyes widened. "*Your* Ned? How long has this been going on, then?"

Gertie grinned. "Go on, you know as how I likes him."

"Yes, I do. I didn't know you got it *that* bad, though."

Gertie lifted her chin. "Who says I got it bleeding bad? I just likes him, that's all."

Ethel swished the carrot around in a tub of water, then attacked it once more with the scrubbing brush. "What about Ned? Does he like you?"

Gertie sighed. That was a question she'd like answered

herself. "I dunno," she admitted. "I never bleeding asked him, did I?"

Ethel stopped scrubbing and looked over her shoulder. "Has he kissed you, then?"

Gertie felt her cheeks growing warm. "Ethel Salter! You know that's not proper."

"Nor is meeting a strange man down in the cellar in the middle of the night, but you did it."

Gertie was beginning to regret ever telling Ethel every bloody thing that had happened to her while her friend was living in London. "That was different," she said huffily. "Ross McBride was much older. Anyway, I knew he wouldn't try any funny stuff."

"He kissed you, though." Ethel went back to scrubbing the carrot. "And he asked you to marry him."

Gertie's eyes misted over as she remembered the husky Scotsman who had been so kind to her. "He was lonely, that's all," she muttered.

"Has he written to you yet?"

"Nah." Gertie did her best to sound as if she couldn't care less. "Nor did I expect him to. More'n likely he's forgotten all about me by now."

"I don't think anyone would ever forget about you," Ethel said stoutly. "Not even Ian."

"You can leave my bloody ex-husband out of this," Gertie said, viciously chopping at the cabbage. "I wish this was his bleeding head."

Ethel let out a shriek. "You're horrible, Gertie. Fancy saying something like that."

"He bloody deserves to have his head chopped up after leaving me alone to bring up two babies all by meself. Ruined me flipping life, he did."

"They're beautiful babies, though," Ethel said, her voice tinged with envy. "I can't believe they're going to be a year old in two months."

"I can bloody believe it. Feels like they've been around a blooming lifetime to me." Gertie scooped up the pieces of cabbage into a colander. "If it wasn't for Doris taking care of the babies for me, and me living here at the Pennyfoot, I don't know what I'd do, that I bloody don't. I'd be on the bleeding street, begging for ha'pennies, I wouldn't be surprised."

"I reckon we'd all be on the street." Ethel tipped the water from the tub down the sink. "You, me, the twins, Mrs. Chubb, even Michel."

"That bugger wouldn't last a bleeding day on the street," Gertie muttered darkly. "I don't know what's bitten him lately, but he's been in a bloody filthy temper for the last two days. If he don't watch out, I'll be chopping his bleeding head off with me knife."

Ethel glanced nervously over her shoulder. "Don't say things like that, Gertie. He might hear you."

"Too bleeding bad if he does." Gertie looked up at the clock that stood on the mantelpiece above the ovens. "Cor blimey, is that the time? Where the blinking 'eck is Doris, then?"

"Exactly what I want to know," said the plump, gray-haired woman who entered the kitchen just then. "I've just come from the dining room, and the tables are still not cleared. Doris should be in here washing up the dishes. Michel is going to throw a fit."

"That's nothing bleeding unusual," Gertie muttered under her breath as the housekeeper marched across the kitchen to the stove.

"Stop your grumbling, Gertie, and see if you can find Doris. Tell her to get to the dining room at once. Ethel, go and start clearing off the rest of the tables. Then get back here and help Doris with the dishes."

"Yes, Mrs. Chubb." Ethel rushed to the door, her long gray skirt swirling about her ankles.

"I haven't finished the bleeding vegetables yet," Gertie said, dumping the colander on the stove. "Michel will be flipping screaming at me if they're not done."

"You leave Michel to me," Mrs. Chubb said grimly.

"Get on out there and find Doris. I can't imagine what's keeping her. It's not like that girl to run off and leave her duties like this."

"How do I know where she bleeding is?" Gertie demanded. "It could take me all blinking afternoon to find her."

"It had better not." Mrs. Chubb folded her arms across her ample bosom and glared at Gertie. "While you're standing here wasting time arguing with me you could be up there looking for her. Now do what you're told for once."

Gertie straightened her spine and glared back. " 'Ere, I'm not a bleeding kid, you know. I'm the mother of twins, I am."

"You're also a housemaid, my girl, and don't you forget it. Now get on with you, before I report you to Madam for being cheeky again."

"Strewth!" Gertie stomped across the kitchen, resentment burning in her breast. "Don't know what's the bleeding matter with everyone around here lately. You're all acting like you've got bloody wasps in your drawers."

Mrs. Chubb opened her mouth and let out a roar that would have silenced the devil himself. "Gertay! That's enough!"

Gertie knew when she'd gone too far. Clenching her teeth, she muttered, "Yes, Mrs. Chubb."

"And straighten that cap. And your petticoat's showing—the hem must be down. Get a needle and stitch it up. I don't know why you have to go around looking like a ragamuffin . . ."

Her voice faded away as the kitchen door closed behind Gertie. Letting out her breath in an explosive snort, Gertie trudged up the steps to the foyer.

She heard the voices before she rounded the top of the stairs. Ned's cheerful tone was unmistakable, as was the confused bellow of Colonel Fortescue.

"Dash it all, my good chap, why can't you speak ruddy English!"

"I am speaking English, Colonel. I tell you, I saw 'em with my very own minces."

"Minces? What the devil is minces, then?"

Gertie hurried toward the two men, shaking her head. Ned loved to confuse the colonel with his Cockney rhyming slang, but the brash doorman hadn't been working at the Pennyfoot long enough to know that Colonel Fortescue could become difficult to handle if pushed too far.

"Mince pies, Guv," Ned was saying as she reached them. He poked his two fingers at the colonel's eyes making the gentleman stagger backward.

"I say, old chap, that's not cricket, you know." The colonel raised his walking cane in a threatening manner. "I'll give you a blasted bonce on the noggin if you don't watch out."

Ned danced around the elderly gentleman, jabbing short punches in the air. "Yeah? You and whose army, then, Guv?"

"The whole damn British Army, that's who. Insolent blighter!" The colonel started stabbing his cane at Ned as if he were brandishing a sword. "I once took on a whole herd of natives, the bastards. I'll soon make short work of a blasted whippersnapper like you."

"Leave him alone, Ned," Gertie said, tugging at the doorman's sleeve. "You'll get in bleeding trouble if you upset him."

"I'm not upsetting him. I'm just having a bit of fun." Ned stopped dancing and dropped his hands. "He likes sparring with me, don't you, Guv?"

The colonel lowered his cane and peered at Ned as if seeing him for the first time. "I do? Oh, yes, old chap, of course I do. Does one good to have a spot of exercise after meals, what?" He turned his bloodshot gaze onto Gertie. "Must say, though, I prefer to wrestle with the ladies, what? What?"

Gertie neatly sidestepped the colonel's outstretched hand. "I think someone's waiting for you in the bar, Colonel," she said, winking at Ned. "He had a dirty great brandy in his hand last I saw him."

"Did he, by Jove? I'd better toddle off, then. Tally ho, and all that rot."

Ned chuckled as the colonel cantered down the hallway like an aging, bow-legged horse. "Weird old geezer, ain't he? Definitely off his rocker, if you ask me."

"He ain't going to get any bleeding better if flipping twerps like you keep teasing him," Gertie said tartly. "You'd better not let Madam catch you bleeding doing that." She pursed her lips and did her best to imitate the King's English. "You're supposed to treat the hotel guests with the proper bleeding respect they deserve."

Ned grinned. "The colonel ain't a guest. He's a bloody liability. He's going to go completely berserk one of these days, you mark my words."

"He already has," Gertie said, lifting the hem of her skirt to inspect her petticoat. "More than once. He almost ran Mr. Baxter through with his sword once."

"Go on," Ned said, his eyes alight with curiosity. "What happened then?"

Gertie shrugged. "Nothing. Mr. Baxter and Arthur, the gent what was doorman before you, they both grabbed him, and he calmed down. But I'd watch him if I was you. You never know with the colonel."

She looked up to find Ned staring at the hem of her petticoat. "Go on, then," he said in the soft voice that always gave her a weird feeling in her stomach, "show us your ankles, then."

She let go of her skirt and shoved her fists into her hips. If she raised her heels just a little bit, she was taller than Ned. It gave her a wonderful sense of power. "You mind your flipping tongue, Ned 'arris, or I'll bleeding mind it for you."

Ned's grin grew wider. "You're bloody beautiful when you're cross, me darlin'."

Gertie came down hard on her heels. "Go on with you. Any more cheek from you, and I'll tell Madam how you treat her guests."

To her surprise, Ned's smile vanished. "I know one guest I'd like to bloody treat, I can tell you."

She could tell from the dreadful look in his eyes that he wasn't joking. "Watcha mean?" she said sharply. "What guest?"

Ned's scowl frightened her. Sometimes he could get such a cruel look on his face. Those were the times when she felt like she didn't know him at all.

"My bloody worst enemy," Ned muttered fiercely, "that's who. I'd like to put him away for good for what he done to me."

"Why, what'd he do to you, then?" Gertie demanded. She didn't really want to hear it, but the look of hatred on Ned's face filled her with a horrible fascination. She had to know what had caused that vicious grimace, no matter how gruesome the story might be. Something told her that the details might just make her bring up her breakfast.

CHAPTER

❦ 5 ❦

"Remember I told you about the time the judge put me in the nick for stealing a watch?" Ned said, staring off into space as if he were watching ghosts of the past.

"Of course I remember." Gertie frowned. "You caught the thief what really stole the watch, and when the bobby came after you, the thief gave you the bleeding watch and ran off."

"And the bobby said as it were me what stole it."

"And the judge put you in prison 'cause he said you looked guilty. Bleeding terrible that was. That judge ought to have to go to the nick hisself for that."

Ned nodded. "Them's my sentiments exactly. Well, what would you say if I told you that bleeding judge was right here, under this very same roof?"

Gertie felt the shock of his words all the way down to

her shiny Oxfords. "Go on," she whispered. "Who is he, then?"

"His name's Lord Sittingdon." Ned just about spat the words out.

Gertie stared at him. "Lord Sittingdon? I didn't know he was a bleeding judge."

Ned uttered a mirthless laugh. "Only the most famous prosecutor in London, ain't he? I ain't the only one what he done it to, neither."

"What, he put someone else in prison for something he didn't do?"

"Not exactly." Ned looked down the hallway then up at the stairs, as if to make sure no one could hear him. Then he leaned closer and said quietly, "Them two women what are staying here, the ones what belong to the Women's Movement?"

Gertie opened her mouth in astonishment. "The suffragettes? Lord Sittingdon put them in prison?"

"I don't know about that. But I heard them talking down the pub last night. They was drinking beer and talking loud enough for the whole village to hear them."

Gertie jiggled her foot up and down with impatience. "What did they say, then?"

"They said as how it was Lord Sittingdon what ordered the terrible treatment they got in prison. He wanted to set an example, so's the rest of 'em would stop making so much trouble. That's why they're down here. They found out he was coming, and they came here to spoil his holiday. 'Cos of what he done to them."

Gertie could feel cold chills chasing down her back. She wasn't sure she wanted to know the gory details of what had happened to the suffragettes, but the thought of carrying such horrifying tales back to the kitchen was too delicious to resist. "What'd he do to 'em, then?" she whispered.

"Gertie Brown! I thought I told you to go and find Doris."

Gertie jumped a foot in the air at the sound of the strident voice bellowing from the top of the kitchen steps. "I was, Mrs. Chubb, honest I was. I was just asking Ned if he'd seen her. I'm on me way up the bleeding stairs right now."

"If you're not down here in less than ten minutes with Doris, then both of you can look for another job."

"Yes, Mrs. Chubb." Gertie leapt for the stairs and rushed up them, tripping over her skirt on the way. Her heart was thumping, but whether it was from her hasty rush upstairs or from the terrifying pictures conjured up in her imagination by Ned's sinister voice she wasn't sure.

One thing she did know. She was going to bloody find out what had happened to the suffragettes while they were in prison if it was the last thing she did.

Doris stood on the tips of her toes and aimed her feather duster at the ornate picture rail above her head. A little puff of exasperation left her lips when she discovered she couldn't quite reach it.

Not that it really mattered. It wasn't her job to dust the upstairs hallway anyway. That was delegated to one of the other housemaids. All she was supposed to do was clean out the suites on the second floor.

She wasn't supposed to be on the top floor at all. In fact, right now she should be in the dining room clearing off the tables. She could feel a quiver in her stomach when she thought about how angry Mrs. Chubb would be if she found out the dishes hadn't been cleared away yet.

Doris had no idea how long she'd been hovering in the hallway of the top floor. Her mind was set on one course only—she was going to talk to Bella DelRay if she had to wait there all afternoon. It would be worth getting into trouble, she assured herself, if she could have a few minutes alone with the celebrated songstress.

She'd waited a very long time for a chance to talk to a real live Variety star, and she wasn't about to let the opportunity slip through her fingers. Bella DelRay might be able to tell her how to get on the stage. If the gods were really smiling on her, the singer might even offer to help her.

Doris near on swooned at the thought. Fancy her being this close to someone who actually sang in the Variety halls of London! Why, Bella DelRay must have met dozens of toffs.

Doris whisked the feather duster along the banisters at the top of the stairs, her imagination painting a glorious picture of her, Doris Hoggins. . . .

She paused, shaking her head in silent protest. No, singing stars didn't have names like Doris Hoggins. They had names like Bella DelRay, Vesta Tilley, or Camille Clifford, the famous Gibson Girl. Them were names everyone remembered.

Doris frowned, trying to think what name she should use. Something dashing, a name no one would ever be able to forget. Dolores Davenport . . . that was a good one.

She whispered it aloud, trying out the delicious sound of it. "Dolores Davenport." She nodded her head in satisfaction. The name sounded just right. So much more glamorous than—

"Doris 'Oggins! Where the bleeding hell have you bin?"

Like the crash of thunder on a serene summer's day, the harsh voice shattered Doris's lovely daydream. She dropped the duster in her fright and almost lost it down the stairs.

"You scared me, Miss Brown," she said breathlessly as Gertie stomped up the stairs toward her. "I didn't see you coming."

"You wouldn't have seen a bloody elephant coming with your bleeding eyes shut like that." Gertie paused at the top of the stairs, breathing heavily as she dug a fist into her side. "Strewth, these blooming stairs will be the death of me." She glared at Doris. "It's your bleeding fault I had to come up 'em. Mrs. Chubb is having a pink fit down there. You'll be bleeding lucky if she doesn't give you the flipping sack."

Doris's heart sank. She must have been up here longer than she thought. "I was just finishing the dusting," she said, giving the banisters another flick for good measure.

"What dusting?" Gertie looked around the hallway. "There ain't bleeding nothing to dust."

"It's the banisters," Doris said timidly. "They take such a long time."

Gertie stopped panting and folded her arms in a fair imitation of Mrs. Chubb. "Oh, yeah? Well, what I want to know is, why are you bleeding dusting up here, anyway? You're supposed to be down in the dining room clearing the tables. And then you're supposed to be in the bloody kitchen bleeding washing them."

Doris gave a guilty start. "I must have got mixed up," she said, sending one last, longing glance at the closed door of Bella DelRay's room. "I'll come down right away."

Muttering to herself, Gertie plodded back down the stairs.

Following close behind, Doris was already forming a new plan to speak to Bella DelRay. So deep in thought was she that she didn't notice Gertie stop dead on the landing of the second floor. Not until she'd plowed into her, that is.

Gertie yelped as the heel of Doris's heavy shoe descended on her toe. Instead of turning on the young girl with a string of curses, however, which was what Doris might have expected, Gertie stood looking down the hallway at the woman coming toward them.

Following the head housemaid's gaze, Doris realized what had caught Gertie's attention. The woman was Lady Katherine, wife of Lord Sittingdon. She was staggering down the hallway, hands outstretched, while tears streamed unchecked down her face.

"You know, Baxter," Cecily murmured, "it really is refreshing to have you seated at your desk while I visit with you. It used to be so frustrating trying to talk to you while you hovered over me whenever I came into the office. I had a permanent crick in my neck from being forced to look up at you all the time. I must confess, I enjoy this informality a great deal more.''

Baxter looked up from the ledger he was studying. ''Since officially I no longer am employed by you, Cecily, we no longer have to observe such strict proprieties, which was the precise reason I left in the first place.''

Cecily grinned at him. ''I thought this day would never come. You were always such a stickler for proprieties.''

His face was expressionless as he gazed at her. ''Perhaps I should remind you that our informality should apply only in private.''

Cecily sighed. ''And I was beginning to have such high hopes for you, Bax.''

His smile delighted her. ''I will do my best not to disappoint you, my dear madam.''

''I have no fear of that.'' Unsettled by the expression in his eyes, she glanced at the ledger opened in front of him. ''I really appreciate having someone do the book work again.''

''I am beginning to doubt my capabilities.'' He gestured with his pen at the almost-blank page. ''There have been no entries in this book since your ex-manager left. Where have you managed to conceal all the invoices and receipts?''

Cecily got up from her chair and opened a drawer in the filing cabinet. ''They are all in here, I think.''

''You think?'' Baxter groaned. ''Never mind. I'll find them. Though heaven knows if I'll be able to make sense of anything.''

Cecily returned to her chair. ''Piffle! You've always managed to handle things admirably, Baxter. You know more about the accounting procedures of this hotel than I do.''

''I have been away so long I'm surprised I remember anything at all.'' He turned a page, shaking his head in dismay. "I have my work cut out for me if I am to get things in order."

"Well, now that I can leave all this in your capable hands, I shall have more time to devote to the problems of the staff." She sighed. "I'm afraid I've rather neglected them lately. Poor Gertie will wish she had made a better choice for godmother to her twins."

Baxter grimaced. "Or godfather, I imagine. Perhaps we can offer to take them off her hands for an afternoon's outing. Do you think she would trust them to us?"

Cecily gave him a smile of absolute pleasure. "You and I with the twins? She'd adore it. And so would I." In all the years she had known Baxter, they had never been on an outing alone together. Of course, they wouldn't be strictly alone, but taking care of babies together could turn out to be an interesting experience.

"Then it's settled. I'll leave it to you to arrange it."

She had no time to consider the intriguing possibilities of such an arrangement, as a sharp rap on the door banished her contemplation. She waited for Baxter to answer, and after a moment's pause, he rose from his chair, calling out, "Yes, who is it?"

The door opened, and Gertie appeared in the opening. Her eyes were wide in her pale face, and she stared at Baxter as if seeing him for the first time.

"What is it, Gertie?" Cecily scrambled to her feet, alarmed by the young woman's expression.

Gertie looked from one to the other, as if not certain to whom she should speak. "Mr. Baxter . . . mum . . ."

Cecily reached for the housemaid's arm and drew her into the office. "Sit down, Gertie, and tell us what is the matter."

Gertie shook her head. "I'm all right, mum. I came to tell you Lady Katherine wants you to send for the doctor. Her husband, Lord Sittingdon . . ." She swallowed and grabbed her throat with her shaking hand. "He's dead, mum." Her voice dropped to a whisper. "He's been bleeding poisoned. And Lady Katherine says it was something he ate from the kitchen what killed him.''

"I've never heard such nonsense in my entire life," Mrs. Chubb angrily declared when Gertie had finished telling her about the way Lady Katherine had carried on. "This kitchen is absolutely spotless. I make good and sure of that. How dare that woman suggest that the food was spoiled. We are very particular here at the Pennyfoot. There isn't anything that goes out of this kitchen that I wouldn't eat myself."

"What if it was something you didn't know about?" Gertie said unhappily.

Mrs. Chubb eyed her with suspicion. "Of course I'd know about it. I know everything that goes out of here. What I want to know is why no one else has been taken ill if the food was spoiled. There are enough people eating the meals. Surely someone else would be ill by now?"

"Maybe no one else ate what Lord Sittingdon ate," Gertie said, wishing she didn't have to tell Mrs. Chubb what was on her mind.

The housekeeper folded her arms across her bosom and glared at Gertie. "All right, my girl, out with it. There's something you're not telling me, isn't there?"

Gertie nodded. "I took a tray up to the Sittingdons' suite last night. Michel made it up for me. P'raps there was something on the tray that didn't go into the dining room."

Mrs. Chubb stared at her for the longest time. Then she said quietly, "Don't tell anyone else what you've told me. Understand?"

Gertie nodded, feeling scared now. She and Michel had their differences, but there were times when he could be really kind. The last thing on earth she wanted to do was get him into trouble. "Do you think I should tell Madam?" she asked nervously as Mrs. Chubb paced around the kitchen with a fierce scowl on her face.

"No, that's something I'd better do. Doris and Ethel

should be in with the dishes any minute. See that they get
them washed and dried as soon as possible.''

"Yes, Mrs. Chubb.''

"And remember what I said. Don't say anything to anyone.''

"Yes, Mrs. Chubb.'' Gertie watched the housekeeper
disappear through the door, a hollow feeling settling into
the pit of her stomach. "I'm bloody sorry, Michel,'' she
whispered.

Phoebe hurried up the steps of the Pennyfoot, folding up
her parasol as she went. She couldn't imagine how she
could have forgotten to ask Cecily about rehearsal time that
morning. Her mind had been slipping quite a bit lately, she
thought worriedly. Surely it was not a sign that she was
growing senile?

The thought depressed her no end. Admittedly she was
a shade over fifty, but that didn't mean she was ready to
give up on life, so to speak. She still had her figure, thanks
to the excruciating bondage of her tightly laced corsets, and
she liked to think that her looks had not faded altogether.

True, she had just about given up on the idea of finding
someone with whom to enjoy her waning years, but she
still looked forward every day to the intriguing possibilities
that awaited her. Lately, however, her days had been sadly
lacking in excitement.

Phoebe reached the top step just as Ned opened the door
with a flourish. She answered his cheerful greeting with a
curt nod and swept past him, her chin in the air. She had
never taken to Cecily's new doorman. He was not in the
least like Arthur, Ned's predecessor. Now there was a gentleman—gracious, charming, and always ready with a
smile. It was really too bad that Arthur had turned out to
be less than worthy of her esteem.

So intent was Phoebe on her thoughts as she crossed the
lobby that she failed to see Colonel Fortescue until he was

almost on top of her. Pulling up sharply, she glared up at him from under the brim of her hat.

"I say, old bean," the colonel bellowed, "that was a close one, what? What?"

"Really, sir," Phoebe muttered. "I do think you could watch where you are going."

"I was watching, by Jove." The colonel smoothed one end of his mustache with his fingers. "It isn't often one gets the chance to chat with such an enchanting creature. I was anxious to waylay you before you could slip away. You are surprisingly swift on your feet, you know."

Phoebe eyed him suspiciously, not certain whether he was attempting to be charming or insulting. "I'm in rather a hurry, Colonel," she said, deciding to give him the benefit of the doubt. "Please excuse me."

"If you insist, old bean." He actually had the audacity to wink at her. "If you're free later on, madam, perhaps you would care to join me in the drawing room for a spot of gin?"

"I never touch the stuff, Colonel. It's very bad for the liver."

"Bad for the liver?" The colonel looked thunderstruck. "How can you say that, madam? Why, that's the stuff that helped build the blasted British Empire. Half of those idiots out in the tropics would have turned tail and run for their lives if they hadn't been three sheets to the wind. That's what gin does for you, old girl. Gives you some dashed spirit."

Phoebe sniffed. "I have quite enough spirit, thank you very much. And I'll thank you not to refer to me as an old girl."

The colonel looked worried. "Oh, no offense, old g— bean. I didn't mean to infer you were ancient, oh, dear, no. Why, to be truthful, I was only thinking how young and sprightly you looked tripping across the lobby just now. Always the picture of grace and beauty, that Mrs. Carter-Holmes, I thought."

The words were music to Phoebe's ears. Her resentment melted away like icicles on a warm roof. "That's very sweet of you to say so, Colonel," she murmured. "Now, if you'll excuse me?"

"Certainly, m'dear." Smiling broadly, the colonel swept her a dramatic bow and stepped aside.

Phoebe waltzed past him, taking care to stay on her toes. She couldn't help wondering if he watched her as she made her way down the hallway to the library. Perhaps the old fool wasn't as strange as some people liked to make out, she mused. He certainly recognized a comely lady when he saw one. Perhaps she had misjudged him all these years. The thought gave her a reason to smile.

CHAPTER

❀ 6 ❀

Alone in the library, Cecily gazed up at the blank space above the fireplace. So often she had sought comfort from her late husband's portrait in times of trouble. It seemed strange not to see it hanging there.

Sighing, she walked over to the French windows and looked outside across the immaculate lawns. Baxter had gone in search of a footman to take a message to Dr. Prestwick. He would be back any minute to chase away her melancholy as he had done so many times in the past.

It was so much nicer to have a live human being in whom to find solace, instead of a mere painting. She remembered then that she hadn't yet told him about the letter from her eldest son, Michael.

With both her sons living abroad, she sometimes felt as if she'd been cast adrift by her family. Since Baxter had never had a family, she wondered if he could ever understand how lonely that had sometimes made her feel.

She and Baxter had shared many an adventure. The close empathy between them had remained steadfast throughout the most trying times, understated though it might have been. She had leaned on him on more than one occasion, and he had supported her, yet never once had he revealed his true feelings until a few short weeks ago.

Even now she wasn't sure where it would all end. For the time being, however, she was content in the knowledge that he cared for her. If it wasn't for this latest catastrophe, she would be sublimely happy.

She was still stunned by the news. A man had died in her hotel—quite possibly from the neglect of someone on her staff. Other people could also be affected by the poison, including herself, for that matter. Though she felt perfectly well, she assured herself.

A tap on the door disturbed her troubled thoughts. Hoping it was Baxter returning from his errand, she crossed the floor on swift feet. She always felt better when in his presence.

It was Mrs. Chubb who waited at the door for her, however. Cecily invited the housekeeper into the room and closed the door behind her. Mrs. Chubb's normally jovial face wore a set expression, warning Cecily that she brought grave news.

"I assume you have heard about the death of Lord Sittingdon," Cecily said, knowing full well that Gertie would have informed the entire kitchen staff by now.

Mrs. Chubb pursed her lips. "Gertie tells me Lady Katherine believes it was food from the kitchen that caused his death."

"We don't know for certain." Cecily lifted her hands in a hopeless gesture and let them drop again. "Though I have to admit it seems likely. Lady Katherine appears to be quite certain her husband ate nothing outside of this hotel."

Mrs. Chubb looked uncomfortable. "Has there been any word of anyone else taken ill?"

"Not as far as I'm aware." Cecily looked closely at the housekeeper. "Do you have any idea what might have happened?"

"No, mum, I really don't. Though I think I should tell you . . ." Her voice faded away, and she looked helplessly at Cecily, making it clear that she was most reluctant to say what was on her mind.

"You must tell me, Altheda," Cecily said gently.

The housekeeper cast her eyes downward. "Well, mum, it appears that Gertie took a tray up to the Sittingdons' suite last night. Apparently Michel prepared it specially for them."

Cecily looked at her sharply. "Michel often prepares a tray for the guests. That just happens to be mere coincidence, no doubt."

"I might have thought so too," Mrs. Chubb said, looking everywhere but at Cecily, "if it hadn't been for my little talk with Michel yesterday morning."

Cecily waited in silence for her to go on.

After a long pause, Mrs. Chubb said reluctantly, "Michel has been banging things around and yelling at the girls lately—even worse than usual. I took him to task on it and asked him what was the matter with him."

Cecily was aware of an unpleasant sensation in the pit of her stomach. "Go on," she said quietly.

"Well, he told me that he'd had a nasty shock when he'd seen Lord Sittingdon. Apparently Michel knew him from when he used to live in London. He didn't tell me any of the details, of course. He never does say much about his past life, but . . ."

Again the housekeeper paused, while Cecily's uneasiness grew. "He was really worried, mum. He said that if Lord Sittingdon recognized him, he could put him away for good." She hesitated a second longer, then voiced the thought that had already formed in Cecily's mind. "I just hope that Michel didn't decide to put the gentleman away first, that's all."

*   *   *

Doris stood at the sink, her back aching and her arms itching from the hot soap suds that clung to her skin. Strands of wispy hair had escaped from her cap and hung limply over her cheeks as steam wreathed around her head.

From behind her she could hear Gertie and Ethel talking in voices too low for her to hear. For once she wasn't paying too much attention to them. All her energy was concentrated on finishing the washing up as soon as possible so that she could make her escape.

She was supposed to lay the tables for afternoon tea, but she planned to take a few minutes to fly up to the top floor and knock on Bella DelRay's door. She had her excuses all ready. She would say that Mrs. Chubb had sent her to collect the empty tray from her room.

It didn't matter that Ethel had already brought it down. Doris would just say that she hadn't seen it come down. She was still kicking herself for not being in the kitchen when the tray had gone up.

If she'd known that the singer had planned on taking all her meals in her room, she told herself, she could have offered to take it up for Ethel. She'd lost her chance now. She'd be stuck in the dining room for the rest of the day, and Mrs. Chubb would never let her take a tray up now.

Her only hope was to dash up there before she went into the dining room, and hope that Bella DelRay wasn't taking an afternoon nap.

Doris thrust a dripping stack of plates onto the draining board with a clatter that brought a curse of protest from Gertie. Doris hardly heard her. She was imagining what she would say to the Variety star when she was finally face-to-face with her.

At last the dishes were done, and Doris took off the big apron that covered her pinafore. "I'm going into the dining room now, Miss Brown," she called out.

To her relief, Gertie was too busy nattering to Ethel to give her more than an impatient wave of her hand. Doris scuttled out the kitchen door and up the steps to the foyer.

Ned was at the front door, talking earnestly to a fashionably dressed woman who seemed in a hurry to get away from him. In fact, she turned her back on him and marched out of the door while he was still talking to her.

Doris was about to fly past him when the woman turned her head to look back at Ned, as if to make sure he wasn't following her. Doris stopped dead in her tracks. She would've recognized that pretty face anywhere. Thrilled at the opportunity fate had thrust upon her, Doris picked up her skirts and fled after Bella DelRay.

Reaching the bottom of the steps, she was just in time to see the singer turn the corner of the hotel, taking the path that led to the rose gardens in the back.

Doris couldn't believe her luck. For a moment or two she'd thought she would have to follow the star down the Esplanade. Excited at the prospect of finally speaking to a real Variety star, Doris sped around the corner of the hotel.

She could see the singer striding across the grass toward the tennis courts. Since Bella wasn't carrying a racquet, Doris reckoned that she wasn't going to play tennis. In fact, before Doris caught up with her, Bella had passed the tennis courts altogether.

Panting with the exertion of her mad dash across the grass, Doris finally got within earshot of the rapidly striding figure. "Miss DelRay!" she called out as the singer headed toward the shrubs bordering the woods. "Can I have a word with you?"

Bella DelRay stopped short, pausing a moment before turning around. With a formidable frown she watched Doris approach. "What do you want?" she demanded as Doris timidly smiled. "What are you following me for? Trying to spy on me, no doubt."

"Oh, no, miss, I wasn't. Honest." Doris shook her head so hard a thick curl shook its pin loose and fell cross her face. Making a grab for it, she pushed it back under her cap.

"Well, then, what were you doing, girl? Answer me! I won't have people following me around and spying on me."

Doris's smile faded at the look of fury on the singer's face. "I . . . I'm sorry, Miss DelRay, I just wanted a word with you, that's all. You're such a famous singer . . . and I want to be a singer, too . . . I just wanted to ask you—" Her breath came out on a sob as her nerves finally crumbled. "I'm sorry," she mumbled, backing away, "I didn't mean no harm, honest."

Thoroughly mortified now, she turned tail, ready to flee from the awful thing she'd done.

"Just a minute!" The singer's imperious voice rang out, freezing Doris to the ground.

She waited, her whole body trembling with anticipation. Nothing in the world could have compelled her to turn around and face her angry accuser.

The silence seemed to go on for an eternity. Doris could hear the seagulls crying to each other across the bay and wished she could be out there with them. Anywhere but standing there waiting for one of her idols to bring the heavens down on her head.

Then Bella DelRay said in quite a different voice, "What is your name, child?"

"Doris, miss," she mumbled.

"Turn around, Doris, and let me look at you."

It took a tremendous effort of will to turn around, but Doris managed it, though she couldn't look the singer in the face. Instead, she stared miserably down at the shiny toes of her shoes peeking out from under the hem of her skirt.

"I'm sorry, child," Bella DelRay said at last, surprising Doris no end. "I shouldn't have shouted at you like that. I'm afraid I haven't been feeling very well, and I get rather irritable when I'm not well."

"Sorry, Miss DelRay," Doris mumbled.

"Well, now, why don't you tell me what it is you want to know?"

Gathering all her courage, Doris looked up. To her immense relief, Bella DelRay was actually smiling at her. The singer did look extremely pale, though, Doris noticed. She had dark circles under her eyes, and her cheeks looked drawn.

"I didn't mean to disturb you," Doris said nervously. "I just wanted to know how I can get to be a singer like you."

Bella gave a dry laugh. "Are you perfectly sure that's what you want?"

Doris nodded fiercely. "All me life I've wanted to be a singer. It's all I ever wanted to do."

"How old are you, child?"

Doris sighed. "I'm almost sixteen." She still had a few months to go but she didn't have to tell her that.

Bella glanced over to the pagoda that sat at the edge of the woods. "Come and sit with me for a minute or two," she said to Doris's wild delight. "I'll tell you all you want to know about becoming a singer."

What followed were the most magical moments of Doris's young life. She just knew she was dreaming, but she was determined to enjoy the dream while it lasted.

Perched on the edge of the bench inside the pagoda, she listened in breathless wonder as Bella recounted some of her more adventurous moments on the stage.

"You have to put up with an awful lot of nonsense," Bella told her after describing the night she'd almost had her clothes ripped off by a zealous fan. "You have to know how to put the buggers in their place, and sometimes you need help to do it. Life on the stage is not all it's cracked up to be, I can tell you."

"But it must be so exciting." Doris breathed, her heart aching with envy. "I can't wait until I can get up there and have all those people listen to me sing."

"They don't always listen to you," Bella said ruefully.

"Sometimes someone will shout out insults, and the audience laughs at him, which makes him shout twice as loud. Then everybody else joins in shouting, and no one can hear what you're singing. Sometimes men think you're the same as the women you're singing about, and think they can do anything they want with you."

Doris stared at her, wide-eyed with excitement. "What about the toffs? Do you meet lots of them?"

Bella shrugged. "Plenty. Most of them are married, though, and just looking for a good time. Once you're a singer, you can forget about your reputation. The minute you set foot on the Variety stage, you're marked as a fallen woman."

"I don't care," Doris said defiantly. "I'm going to be a singer, and nothing is going to stop me."

Bella looked sad as she shook her head. "Well, I can see you got your heart set on it. I was like that myself at your age. You might as well give it a try and get it out of your system."

"How do I do it, though?" Doris said, leaning forward so as not to miss a single word the singer told her.

"There isn't any trick to it," Bella said carelessly. "You just go from door to door, begging for a chance. If you're lucky, you'll get someone who's more interested in your voice than your body."

Doris felt her cheeks grow hot. No one had ever talked to her like that before. Like she was a grown woman. It was wonderful. She couldn't wait to get back and tell Daisy all about it, although her twin would most likely tell her she was bonkers to want to go on the stage after everything Bella had told her.

"The most important question, of course," Bella said, staring thoughtfully at Doris's burning face, "is can you sing?"

Doris nodded. "Everyone tells me I can." She told Bella about the time she'd sung on the stage at the Pennyfoot. "Madam says I can do it again soon. Mrs. Carter-Holmes, she's the one what puts on the entertainment here, says as how I have to sing something proper if I sing again. She says I shocked everyone singing a Variety song. But that's the only kind of song I like to sing.''

Bella grinned. ''Spoken like a real trouper. Tell you what.'' She leaned forward and patted Doris's hand. ''Wait until I'm feeling a little better, then you can come to my suite and sing for me. I should tell you your voice won't be fully developed for at least another year or two, but if you show promise, I'll do what I can to help you.''

She waited for Doris's shriek of delight, then added wryly, ''If I'm still in the business by then.''

''Oh, thank you, Miss DelRay.'' Doris sobbed, unable to contain her tears of joy any longer. ''I don't know how I can thank you enough—''

''You can call me Bella,'' the singer said, rising to her feet. To Doris's dismay, she uttered a little gasp and flung out a hand to steady herself.

Doris rose swiftly, thoroughly alarmed at the sudden pallor in Bella's face. ''Are you all right, Miss DelRay?''

''I will be, as soon as I'm lying down.'' Bella swayed, then held out her hand. ''Come, if you want to thank me, help me back to my suite. I'm feeling a little giddy.''

''Yes, Miss DelRay. I'll be most happy to help.'' Eagerly Doris took hold of her arm.

''Bella,'' the singer muttered. ''Call me Bella.''

''Bella,'' Doris said, anxiously guiding the voluptuous woman down the steps of the pagoda. Praying that nothing bad would happen to the singer before she could fulfill her promise to help her, Doris stoically supported Bella's considerable weight all the way back to the hotel.

Once there, Bella insisted that she could climb the stairs alone. Doris watched her, however, until she had staggered around the corner at the top of the landing.

Something was very wrong with Bella DelRay, she thought worriedly as she fled down the hallway to the dining room. She could only hope that the singer would recover from whatever ailed her, and soon.

She couldn't wait to sing for the star and win her approval. And she was quite sure Bella would approve of her singing. Doris simply wouldn't consider anything less.

Dr. Prestwick arrived later that afternoon, looking unusually grave. He greeted Cecily with a little less warmth than usual, and barely acknowledged Baxter's presence at all.

"I have arranged for someone to fetch the deceased late this evening," Prestwick told Cecily as she accompanied him up the stairs. "I thought it better to transfer the body while your guests are occupied in the dining room."

"That is very thoughtful of you, Kevin. Thank you." Aware of the tension between them, she paused at the door of Lord Sittingdon's suite. "I do hope I haven't upset you," she added quietly.

He gave her a cursory glance. "Of course not, Cecily. I have the deepest regard for you, as you well know. I value our friendship a great deal."

"You seem put out. Are you by any chance resenting my choice of a partner?"

Prestwick shrugged. "I'm afraid your manager and I have never had much time for each other. I daresay I can put up with him for your sake, however. After all, we shall no doubt be seeing a great deal of each other, now that he has returned to Badgers End."

"No doubt," Cecily said evenly. She was tempted to point out that it was none of Kevin Prestwick's business whom she chose as a partner, but prudence dictated that she refrain.

"Well, I suppose I had better get on with this unpleasant task," Prestwick said briskly. "I need to examine the body before it is moved. I'll inform you of my findings before I leave."

"Very well." Cecily matched his official tone. "I have

moved Lady Katherine to another room. I will notify her of your arrival.''

"Thank you.''

As she turned to leave him, he said softly, "I wish you both well, Cecily.''

She glanced back at him over her shoulder. "Thank you, Kevin.'' What would he say, she wondered, if he knew that her relationship with Baxter went beyond business? Would he still wish them well? She rather doubted it.

CHAPTER

❁ 7 ❁

Returning to the foyer, Cecily found two of her guests waiting for her at the foot of the stairs. Winnie Atkins and Muriel Croft greeted her avidly as she approached them.

"Is it true Lord Sittingdon has died?" Winnie asked, speaking in a low, hoarse voice. "We've heard rumors, of course, but no one will tell us any of the details."

Her dark eyes gleamed in her gaunt face. Her sunken cheeks and parched lips made her look like an elderly woman, though Cecily knew she was not yet thirty years old.

Silently praising her loyal staff for obeying her orders not to discuss the death above stairs, Cecily pondered how best to answer the question.

Sooner or later everyone would know that the aristocrat had died. Rumors would fly fast and furious unless she settled the matter. There didn't seem to be any harm in admitting his death, as long as she didn't reveal the cause.

"I'm afraid it's true," she said, keeping her voice down. "I would ask you, however, not to spread the story about. There is no need to spoil the other guests' holiday with such depressing news."

"Oh, we won't say anything," Muriel whispered loudly. She was a good six inches shorter than her friend and kept darting little glances up at the taller woman, as if uncertain if she should speak at all.

"What did he die of, then?" Winnie asked, one hand straying to her long, scrawny neck, which she'd done her best to conceal with her French lace collar.

"I haven't discussed that with the doctor," Cecily said evasively.

Winnie nodded. "Not that it's of much importance now, I suppose."

"As long as he's really dead, praise the Lord," Muriel muttered.

Cecily stared at the woman. "I beg your pardon?"

"You'll have to forgive us, Mrs. Sinclair," Winnie said, sending a dark look at Muriel that clearly warned her to guard her tongue. "I'm afraid we cannot be sad to hear of Lord Sittingdon's passing. It is because of that man that we suffered so in prison. He was responsible for our present weakened state of health."

"I'm sorry," Cecily said, shocked by this revelation. "I had no idea . . ."

"His treatment of us was quite inhuman," Winnie continued, as if Cecily hadn't spoken. "In his desire to break our spirit and teach our sisters a lesson, he was very nearly the death of us. It will be a good many years before we shall forget our suffering at the hands of that monster."

Muriel shivered. "I shall never forget. As long as I live, I won't. Justice has been done, I would say."

"I don't know what to say," Cecily murmured. Much as she sympathized with the women and supported their cause, the premature death of any human being was a tragedy.

Even as the wife of a military man she had felt a deep compassion for the fallen, whether they were friend or foe. She could never forget that somewhere each one had someone mourning him. The somewhat callous attitude of the suffragettes unsettled her.

"Well, it isn't something one cares to talk about much," Winnie said, glancing about her. "We don't want to take the chance of discouraging other women from fighting for our noble cause."

"No, indeed, we don't," Muriel echoed fervently.

"It is difficult enough to convince some women that desperate measures are necessary if we are to succeed." Winnie tossed her head. "We will do whatever we have to do to make the powers that be sit up and take notice."

"Indeed we will," Muriel vowed.

"Very commendable," Cecily said, wondering just what lengths these intense women were prepared to go in the name of the cause.

"Well, thank you for enlightening us, Mrs. Sinclair," Winnie said brightly. "We had come here this week to confront the barrister and tell him exactly what we thought of his brutal treatment, but now we shall be saved the trouble."

"We would like to offer our condolences to the widow, however," Muriel said, with a nervous glance at Winnie.

"Yes, of course," Winnie hastily agreed.

"I'll convey your sympathy," Cecily said, still finding it difficult to accept what she had heard. Lord Sittingdon, it would seem, had concealed more than one unsavory facet of his character.

She watched the two women drift off, trying not to imagine what horrors they had suffered that had so emaciated their bodies. She was rather glad she hadn't learned of Lord Sittingdon's part in their ordeal before his death. She might even have been tempted to deny him a suite at the Pennyfoot Hotel.

She was uncomfortably aware that had she been in the unfortunate shoes of Winnie Atkins or Muriel Croft, she too might have felt less distress at his death.

As it was, no matter how she felt about the man, the fact remained that he had died, under suspicious circumstances, right here in the hotel. What was more, at least two of her guests, as well as a member of her staff, had good reason to celebrate that fact.

Cecily found Baxter waiting for her when she returned to the library. He'd apparently requested afternoon tea, since a large tea tray sat on the low table in front of the fireplace.

Eyeing the three-tiered plate of delicate sandwiches and iced petit fours, Cecily uttered a sigh of pleasure. "I have to admit, Baxter, food can be such a dear comfort in times of trouble."

"*I* was rather anticipating being of service in that particular capacity," Baxter said, sounding affronted. "Unless the charming Dr. Prestwick has already eased your distress."

Cecily hid a smile as she seated herself in the armchair. "Jealousy does not become you, Baxter. Particularly when there is no need for it."

He sat down rather abruptly in the matching chair, looking as if he had just swallowed a rather nasty dose of cod-liver oil. "I never have liked that man," he muttered.

Since this was not news to Cecily, she ignored the comment. "I will be interested to hear what Kevin has to say about the cause of death," she said, reaching for the jug of cream. "I'm hoping he will have changed his opinion about the food poisoning."

"He could well be mistaken." Baxter yawned, apparently bored with the conversation. "There isn't a man alive who hasn't made a mistake now and again. I'm quite sure Prestwick is as fallible as the rest of us."

"No doubt." Cecily poured a minute amount of cream into each bone china cup, then used the silver tongs to add a lump of sugar. "His opinion, however, is based on years of learning and experience. That must surely leave less room for error, does it not?"

Baxter was silent while she poured out the tea from the silver teapot. When she handed him the cup and saucer, however, he took it with the dry comment, "Your tiresome habit of rising to Dr. Prestwick's defense can be quite irritating at times, Cecily."

"As is your unwarranted resentment of him." She offered him a tea plate, but he declined with a brief shake of his head. "I have no intention of arguing the point, however. I have more serious topics to discuss." She reached for an egg and cress sandwich and bit into it.

"Now you have my complete and undivided attention."

She finished her sandwich first, then said quietly, "I have to admit I'm deeply concerned about this business with Lord Sittingdon."

His expression changed immediately. "I am well aware of that. You have had more than your share of anxiety over the past few years. Perhaps it is time to start thinking of retiring from the stress of all this. The hotel business is no life for a woman."

Cecily sighed. "You were doing quite well until that last comment. My prospective retirement may become a moot point, however."

Baxter paused in the act of raising his cup to his lips. "What exactly do you mean?"

"I'm very much afraid that we might lose the Pennyfoot. As we both know, if the death of Lord Sittingdon was due to food poisoning, we'll be held liable. Always supposing it was a case of accidental poisoning."

He frowned at her, his concern revealed in the grave depths of his eyes. "Supposing?"

Cecily chose a fairy cake with pink icing. "Last night,"

she said, after nibbling on the edge of it, "Michel prepared a tray for Lord Sittingdon."

"Michel prepares a tray for a great many guests. That doesn't mean he intentionally poisons them. If something was wrong with the food on the tray, I'm quite certain that Michel would have been unaware of it."

Cecily finished the cake, wondering how she could enjoy the tasty tidbit when she had no appetite. "I would have assumed so, too, if it were not for something Mrs. Chubb told me. Apparently Michel has had some sort of dealings with Lord Sittingdon."

"Dealings?"

Cecily nodded. "Unfortunate dealings, by the sound of it. According to Mrs. Chubb, Michel was deathly afraid that Lord Sittingdon would recognize him. He told Mrs. Chubb that if that happened, he could well be put away for the remainder of his life."

"I assume he meant imprisoned."

"Whatever he meant, the fact is, he had a very good reason for wanting to be rid of Lord Sittingdon."

"And the opportunity to achieve those ends," Baxter added soberly.

Cecily stared unhappily at her cup, heedless of the tea growing cold. "If Michel did poison Lord Sittingdon, he will be guilty of murder. If not, and it was accidental, we will be guilty of negligence. Either way, it looks as if we are facing a grave situation."

Baxter put his cup back down on its saucer. "If you suspect Michel of murdering Lord Sittingdon, we are obliged to inform the constabulary."

Cecily looked up, jolted out of her preoccupation. "You know very well that I shall not implicate a member of my staff without strong cause. All of this is merely conjecture, of course. We have not a shred of evidence to support it. Michel may have a tainted past, but I cannot imagine him capable of such a dreadful deed."

"Michel is unpredictable, and has a violent temper. I

wouldn't discount any possibility if his security were to be threatened.'' Baxter shook his head. "I know how worried you are about all this, but I can't help feeling that you are borrowing trouble. That isn't like you, Cecily.''

She smiled at him. "Maybe I am overreacting. Perhaps it is Michael's letter that is making me overly sensitive.''

Baxter looked wary. "You've heard from Michael?''

She looked down at her hands, reluctant to let him see her pain. "The baby was born a month ago.''

After a short pause, he said quietly, "Congratulations, my dear madam. You are, without doubt, the youngest-looking grandmother I have yet to meet.''

His voice had echoed his apprehension, and she sensed the unspoken question behind his comment. "They are not coming home from Africa,'' she said quietly. "In fact, I think it is most unlikely that I shall ever meet my grandson. I don't think Simani will ever forgive me for my unwillingness to accept her as Michael's wife.''

Baxter leaned forward and covered her hand with his. "I'm so sorry, Cecily. I wish there was something comforting I could say.''

She managed to shrug with a semblance of indifference. "I brought it upon myself, of course. It is too late now to waste time on regrets.''

"You still have Andrew.''

She looked up with a wry smile. "I haven't heard from Andrew in several weeks. No doubt he has a woman in his life with whom to occupy his time.''

"That is natural, I suppose.''

"I know I shouldn't resent it, Bax, but I do. I sometimes feel I have been abandoned by my family.''

"I was rather hoping to fill that void myself.''

She smiled at him, reminding herself how lucky she was to have him there beside her. She had come so close to losing him too.

A light tap on the door brought Baxter to his feet. As Cecily expected, Dr. Prestwick stood on the threshold, his face expressionless when Baxter opened the door.

"I just stopped by to inform you that I have completed my examination," he said, when Cecily invited him in. He stood with his back to the fireplace, his hands clasped behind his back. For an instant he reminded Cecily of James, who had stood much the same way during the cold winter months.

Then he shattered her thoughts by saying, "I'm sorry, Cecily. I must inform you that it is my considered opinion that Lord Sittingdon was poisoned. Under the circumstances, I feel I should conduct a postmortem examination, which I shall have to do in my office, of course."

"I suppose that means the constable will have to be informed," Baxter said sharply.

"That depends on the results of the examination."

"And Lady Katherine, I assume," Cecily said, feeling her spirits sink even lower.

"Precisely." Prestwick gave her a sympathetic look. "I have given her something to help her sleep, since she is rather distraught at present. I imagine when she recovers sufficiently she will decide whether or not she wishes to press charges against the hotel."

Although she had been expecting as much, the blow was almost too much to bear. Cecily sank slowly down on her chair, feeling as if her life blood were being drained from her body.

The doctor took a small step toward her, but Baxter deliberately and rather rudely pushed in front of him. Taking Cecily's hand in his, Baxter patted it gently. "Bear up, Cecily. All is not lost yet."

Prestwick shrugged, then strode to the door and opened it. "All we can hope for now," he said, looking back at her, "is that no one else becomes ill with food poisoning. If that happens, I hate to think of the consequences."

He closed the door firmly behind him, and the sound was like a death knoll in Cecily's heart.

*   *   *

"Come on," Gertie said urgently as Ethel dawdled in the pantry. "We're going to bloody miss them suffragettes if you don't get a bleeding move on."

"I've got to fill the milk jugs first, haven't I," Ethel said, her voice muffled behind the door. "They won't have left yet. They were still eating their lemon soufflé when I left the dining room."

"Well, bleeding hurry up. We don't want them to know we was waiting for them." Gertie looked up at the clock. "It's going to be bleeding dark soon. We'll look blinking stupid going out for a walk along the Esplanade in the flipping dark."

"Keep your hair on, I'm coming." Ethel emerged from the pantry and dragged off her apron. "Where are the babies, then? I thought we were going to take them for a walk."

Gertie shook her head. "Nah, Daisy wanted to take them early. She said they don't sleep proper if they're out too late."

Ethel raised her eyebrows. "You aren't half lucky, Gertie, to have someone like Daisy take care of them babies. You could never have afforded a nanny for them."

" 'Course I couldn't." Gertie headed for the door. "Only toffs have nannies, anyway. I wouldn't bleeding know what to do with one if I had one."

"Same as you do with Daisy, I reckon. Let her do all the work."

Gertie scowled at her friend. " 'Ere, you saying I don't look after me blinking nippers? Daisy likes taking care of them. I have to bleeding fight her to get them back half the bloody time."

"I know you love them and want to take care of them." Ethel led the way up the stairs. "I just think that sometimes you're spoiled, not having to worry about them all the time like other mothers."

"Other mothers have bleeding husbands what look after their wives, so they don't have to bloody work." Gertie stomped up the steps behind Ethel, still scowling at her friend's back. "I'm not so bleeding lucky, am I?"

Ethel paused at the top of the stairs, waiting for Gertie to join her. "If Ian came back again, would you marry him all over again?"

"Not bleeding likely." Gertie came to a halt, struggling to catch her breath. "I already blinking married him once, didn't I? At least, I thought I did. I wasn't to know he was already bleeding married. He don't get no flipping second chance, I can tell you."

She jumped as Ethel nudged her painfully in the ribs. "Well, there's Ned over there. Why don't you go out with him? You need a bit of fun now and again. Keeps you young, so they say."

"Yeah?" Gertie sent a sly glance over at Ned, hoping he was watching her. "I don't need no bloody man to keep young. Me nippers do that for me."

Ned looked over their way and raised his hand in a cheerful greeting. His appreciative whistle echoed across the lobby as they crossed the carpet to the door.

"Oo, 'ark at him," Ethel said, holding onto her hat as she stepped out into the fresh sea breeze. "Cheeky bugger, isn't he?"

"You don't know the half of it."

"Go on." Ethel nudged her again. "Did he try to touch you, then?"

"I'd have bleeding knocked him on his arse if he had," Gertie said indignantly. "No flipping man ain't ever going to touch me again."

"What if you got married again?"

Reaching the bottom of the steps, Gertie lifted her chin to breathe in the salt-seasoned air. "Who'd bleeding have me, what with two blinking kids an' all?"

"Ross McBride wanted to marry you," Ethel reminded her. "I bet you're sorry now you didn't accept."

As always, Gertie got a quivery feeling in her stomach at the mention of the Scotsman's name. "Go on with you," she said, setting off down the street, "can you bleeding imagine me married to a man what wears a flipping skirt?"

Ethel's laughter peeled out, and after a moment Gertie joined in. There was no use moping about Ross McBride. He'd come to Badgers End for the bagpipe contest, stolen her heart in the few days he'd been there, and then he was gone.

It was her own bleeding fault for turning him down. She'd been too scared to go off to live with him in Scotland. She couldn't blame him for not keeping his promise to write to her. He'd probably forgotten all about her by now. He couldn't know that she'd lain awake many a night wishing she'd had the guts to go with him. Now it was too bleeding late.

CHAPTER

❋ 8 ❋

"Come on," Gertie said to Ethel, "we'll go as far as the Punch and Judy tent and then we'll turn around. We should meet them bloody suffragettes on the way back."

They were actually almost back at the hotel before Winnie Atkins and Muriel Croft came wandering out of the door, talking earnestly to each other.

Gertie grinned as she caught sight of them. "There they are," she said, tugging on Ethel's arm. "Let's go and talk to them."

"Do you think they'll tell us what happened to them in prison?" Ethel said, sounding nervous as they hurried along the street to meet the other women.

"I dunno. All we can do is bleeding ask."

"I don't know if I really want to know now." Ethel slowed her pace. "After all, Gertie, it's really none of our business."

" 'Course it's our bloody business." Gertie looked back at her with an impatient frown. "We want to know more about the New Women's Movement, don't we? How can we bleeding help if we don't know everything what goes on? You was the one what flipping suggested we pretend to bump into them out here, so's we could talk without anyone else listening, wasn't you?"

"I know, but what if it's really horrible what happened to them?" Ethel's face turned pale. "What if it could happen to us?"

Gertie snorted. "Don't be bleeding daft, Ethel Salter. That happened in London, didn't it? We're not in flipping London, are we? At least, we bleeding wasn't the last time I looked."

"Shush," Ethel said urgently, sending an anxious look past Gertie's shoulder, "here they come."

Gertie drew in a long breath, then plastered a smile on her face. She wasn't about to admit it to Ethel, but her tummy felt like it had worms crawling around in there. She couldn't imagine what awful horrors had befallen the two scrawny-looking women. She could only hope that she wouldn't be sick right in front of them when they told her.

Turning around to face the suffragettes, she called out to them. "Well, look who's here. I was just telling my friend about you two."

Winnie looked as if she would keep on walking, but Muriel came to a reluctant halt. Her eyes looked enormous under the large flat brim of her black hat. "Hello, Gertie," she said. "It's nice to see you again."

"We can't hang around too long," Winnie said, giving Muriel a hard look. "We're supposed to be down the pub in less than half an hour."

"You meeting someone down there, then?" Gertie asked, wondering who it could be.

The two women exchanged glances. "No, of course not," Winnie said gruffly. "I just meant that we have to get there soon, or it will be time to turn around and come back.''

"You're going into the George and Dragon on your own, without an escort?" Ethel said, her eyes widening in awe of this daring.

"There's no law that says we can't." Winnie's voice was crisp, daring them to argue.

"Oo, I know," Ethel said hurriedly. "I just wondered what people would think, that's all."

"We want them to think. That's the whole idea." Winnie tossed her head. "We have as much right down there as the men. Just let them try to stop us going in there." She took hold of Muriel's arm. "Come on, Muriel, we have to go."

"Wait a minute," Gertie said, moving over to block their path. "I was talking to Ned the doorman today, and he told me as how Lord Sittingdon was the one what treated you so bad while you was in prison."

Muriel's face turned a dark red, while Winnie's expression froze. "Ned talks too much," she said shortly.

"Nah, he only talks to me, 'cos we're good friends, like." Gertie looked up and down the deserted Esplanade. In spite of the empty street, she lowered her voice to a confidential whisper. "He told me they did terrible things to you in prison. What was it like in there, then?"

Muriel whimpered, and Winnie gave her arm a little shake. "We were flogged, tortured, and humiliated in the most disgusting way imaginable," she said, her voice harsh with bitterness. "When we refused to eat, we were forced to swallow filth. As you can imagine, we don't like to talk about it much. The memories are too painful."

"Well," Gertie said, disappointed she didn't get all the gruesome details, "you don't have to worry about that old sod no more." She paused for effect, then in a dramatic voice announced, "He's bleeding dead, ain't he?"

She was sadly disappointed in the suffragettes' indifference.

"I know," Winnie said quietly. "And good riddance."

Gertie jumped when Ethel nudged her in the back. "We're not supposed to talk about it," she muttered.

"I wasn't bleeding going to," Gertie said, scowling at her. She turned back to Winnie. "What we really want to know is all about that Women's Movement. Me and Ethel want to join, don't we, Ethel?"

Ethel look startled, but much to Gertie's surprise, didn't argue.

Winnie's expression changed, and she looked at both girls with renewed interest. Then she drew her thin lips back in a smile that seemed more sinister than friendly. "Well, in that case," she said softly, "why don't you both come down to the George and Dragon Inn with us? We could certainly use your help."

"Help with what?" Ethel demanded, while Gertie's stomach started churning with excitement.

Winnie's ugly smile got wider. "Help us storm the bastions of male supremacy, of course. I think you'll find it quite interesting."

"Oh, we couldn't," Ethel said quickly.

Gertie stared at her in exasperation. "Yes, we bloody can."

"No, we can't."

"Why not?"

"Because I have to get home to my Joe. He'll be wondering where I am."

"He won't even notice you're not there." Gertie folded her arms, reluctant to give up this chance for some excitement. "You said yourself as how he spends all his bleeding time in the fields."

"Not in the dark, he doesn't. He'll be on the way home now and expecting me there." Ethel gave Gertie an accusing look. "Anyhow, what about your babies? You can't just go off and leave them without telling Daisy where you're going."

"Don't be such a bleeding spoilsport, Ethel. You never used to be such a bloody crybaby."

"I never used to be married, neither."

"Ladies!" Winnie held up her hand. "Please don't argue on our account. In any case, I doubt if you could make much difference here in this tiny village. It is London where we make the most impact."

"Then why are you bothering with the bleeding George and Dragon?" Gertie demanded.

Winnie shrugged. "As long as we are here, we might as well try to educate the local villagers."

Gertie laughed. "You won't learn that lot nothing. They're all the same. They think women are only good for keeping their houses clean and their beds warm."

"Which is why we must show them how wrong they are. All we ask is that they observe the same morals and standards they expect from women. If it's wrong for women to drink in a public bar, why isn't it wrong for men? A simple question, wouldn't you say?"

"Well," Ethel said, "it's different for them, isn't it?"

"Exactly. But can you tell me why?"

Ethel looked confused. "That's the way it's always been, I s'pose."

"And that makes it right? That women should be persecuted, ignored, ridiculed, and abused, just because they were born as females instead of males? Where in God's name is the justice in that?"

Winnie began pacing up and down, emphasizing her words with grand, sweeping gestures of her hands. "Women are human beings, with minds, brains, and creative talent, just like men. Yet where are the great women artists, musicians, composers, explorers, scientists?

"Only in the last century have we seen women in some of those roles, and pitiably few at that. Why? Because it isn't considered seemly for women to follow such pursuits, or even to desire them. Therefore it is almost impossible for women to follow their dreams."

She stopped pacing and flung her hand out toward the

ocean. With her face tilted toward the darkening sky, her voice rang out across the deserted sands.

"Until men recognize and accept that we are not here to serve them and that there must be equality between us, until we are allowed to vote in Parliament, until all men agree that we must share the same morals and obligations, we must fight for those dreams with our last ounce of energy and our last breath. We must continue to demonstrate, to bring recognition to our cause. We owe it to our sisters, and to all the future women of this earth."

For a moment or two, no one moved in the profound silence that followed Winnie's impassioned speech.

Then Muriel's squeaky voice piped out nervously, "Votes for women!"

"Oo 'eck," Ethel muttered.

Gertie couldn't even speak. She felt something stir deep inside her, something strange and wonderful. The feeling seemed to grow, becoming stronger, as she thought about what Winnie had said.

Could it really be possible that women and men could be treated alike? That women could actually be allowed to do the same things as men, and not have to be their flipping slaves anymore?

Gertie heaved a great big sigh. What a bleeding lovely dream.

"I'm sorry you can't join us," Winnie said, beginning to drag Muriel down the street by her sleeve. "We have work to do and no more time to waste."

Gertie barely noticed them leaving, so engrossed was she in what she'd just heard.

"Are you all right?" Ethel asked as they began walking up the Esplanade toward the hotel. "You look sort of funny."

"I was thinking." Gertie came to a halt, her heart thumping with excitement. "I know we can't go to flipping London to join the Movement, but there's nothing to stop us from carrying on the bleeding fight right here in Badgers

End. After all, we have to bloody start somewhere.''

Ethel's eyes grew wide. "What do you mean?"

"I mean, we should plan our own flipping demonstration. Make all these bleeding twerps of men sit up and take notice, that's what."

"We can't," Ethel said, sounding horrified. "My Joe would never allow it."

Gertie sighed. "Ethel, if things were the way they should be, like Winnie Atkins said, Joe wouldn't have no bleeding say in it. You could do what you bloody well liked."

"I do what I like now."

Gertie laughed. "You couldn't go down to the pub tonight."

"Well, no, but—"

"What if it were Joe what wanted to go down to the bleeding pub? Wouldn't he just go?"

"Well, yes, I s'pose so, but—"

"So why can't you?"

"Well, it's diff—" Ethel stared at her for a long time. "What are you going to do?" she asked at last.

"I dunno yet. It'll have to be something good." Gertie smiled. "It'll be like getting back at bloody Ian for everything he bleeding done to me. Winnie Atkins is right. We don't have to put up with all that bleeding shit from men. Women should have rights, too. After all, if it weren't for flipping women, there wouldn't be any bloody men."

Ethel frowned. "Why not?"

" 'Cos women are the ones what have bleeding babies, aren't they."

"They can't have them without men," Ethel pointed out.

For once Gertie didn't have an answer.

Cecily arose the next morning with only one small hope to brighten her spirits. So far she had received no word of any new illnesses. She prayed that meant that Lord Sittingdon's death was an isolated incident.

She would have to face Lady Katherine some time that

day, she told herself as she washed her face in the luke-
warm water that Doris had brought up earlier. It would not
be a pleasant visit, by any means. She hoped that Baxter
would agree to accompany her for support.

She dabbed her face on a towel, carrying it with her to
the window. How she loved looking out across the gardens
every morning, she thought as she drew aside the heavy
damask curtains.

Enormous white clouds scudded across the sky this
morning, sending dark shadows racing across the pristine
lawns. The sun played hide and seek among the topiaries
and glinted briefly on the heavy dew that still clung to the
dark green leaves.

She looked toward the rose garden, where the last of the
marigolds grew thick along the path. They were John's favorite flower, their wide splash of brilliant orange keeping
the dying summer alive.

Thinking of John, Cecily wondered if he'd kept watch
over his hydrangeas during the night. Flowers were like
pets to the reticent gardener, and he mourned the passing
of each one.

She couldn't help smiling. John was as much a part of
the hotel gardens as the trees that grew there. She could
almost imagine his image carved out in one of the topiaries.

She was about to turn away when she caught sight of a
figure dressed in pale blue, walking unsteadily across the
grass by the tennis courts. The woman was too far away
for Cecily to recognize her. In any case, the white parasol
she carried hid her face from view.

No doubt one of the guests enjoying the last warm days
of summer, Cecily thought as she returned to her toilet.
Winter would be upon them before they knew it.

She wound her hair into its customary bun and pinned it
firmly in place. Catching sight of her face in the mirror,
she was appalled to see the lines that worry had etched
there. She really had to stop fretting about everything, she
told herself firmly.

Determinedly, she set her face in a smile. There, that was better. She had a great deal to be thankful for, after all. She no longer had to face these problems alone. She had a business partner to share her troubles with, and if the gods were willing, one day he could well be her marriage partner.

Keeping the smile firmly tacked in place, she left her suite and descended the stairs.

CHAPTER

❄ 9 ❄

By an ill stroke of luck, Cecily ran into Colonel Fortescue at the foot of the stairway. "Good morning, old girl," he bellowed as soon as he saw her. "Just the person I need to see, what, what?"

Cecily hid her dismay behind the smile. "Good morning, Colonel. What can I do for you?" She couldn't help noticing that the elderly gentleman had not buttoned his waistcoat correctly. The right side at the top overlapped the left by a good two inches, leaving the rest of it bunched unbecomingly across his chest. She found it most distracting.

"You must have someone set a trap for that blasted beast lurking in the hotel grounds." The colonel shot a hunted look over his shoulder, then leaned forward. His hand waved vaguely in front of his face as he whispered hoarsely, "Saw it last night, old bean. Was going to go after the dratted thing with my rifle until I remembered I didn't have any shot. Dashed awkward, that was, what?''

Cecily had long ago discovered that the shortest route to a quick escape from the eccentric gentleman was to humor him. ''Where did you see it, Colonel?''

''Down by the blasted tennis courts. Yes, that was it. Shook me up so badly, I had to have a strong tot of the old mother's ruin, don't you know.''

Cecily had already surmised as much, since the smell of gin on his breath had almost asphyxiated her. ''I'm sorry, Colonel,'' she said soothingly. ''I'll have John take care of it right away.''

''Yes, well, tell that old fool to be careful. Dashed dangerous those things are. Don't like to be taken by surprise, you know.''

''I'll be sure to tell him,'' Cecily said, doing her best to edge past him.

The colonel, however, was not going to allow her to escape so easily this time. He wedged himself between the stairs and the hallway, leaving no room to maneuver gracefully around him. ''I thought about taking my sword to it, by Jove,'' he announced. ''A dab hand at sword play, if I may say so.''

''So you've told me,'' Cecily murmured. She cast a desperate eye down the hallway in the hope that someone might rescue her. Even Ned was nowhere to be seen in the lobby, which was unusual. It wasn't yet time for his mid-morning break. Ned was not usually one to desert his post.

Aware that the colonel was talking to her, she made an effort to pay attention.

''—there I was, face-to-face with the damned thing. Couldn't do a dashed thing about it, of course. My sword was back in the tent, and my blasted trousers were down around my ankles.''

Cecily blinked. ''I beg your pardon?''

The colonel coughed loudly. ''Sorry, old girl. No disrespect and all that rot. They don't have commodes out in the jungle, you know. Have to take your chances in the bushes, what?''

"Yes," Cecily said faintly. "I know."

" 'Course you do, old girl. Keep forgetting you were out in the tropics with that husband of yours. Dashed sight more awkward for the ladies, what? All that blasted crouching and bending—"

"Colonel, I really do have to get along . . ."

"What? Oh, beg pardon, old bean. Didn't mean to embarrass you, you know." Fortescue lifted a hand as if about to give her a hearty slap on the back, thought better of it, and pulled his hand back.

"Anyway, there I was, trapped by my blasted jodhpurs, so to speak. Not a dashed native in sight. Those bastards were never there when you needed them."

Out of the corner of her eye Cecily saw Doris turn the corner at the top of the kitchen steps. She was carrying a large tray of silverware to the dining room.

"Excuse me, Colonel," Cecily murmured, "I must have a word with my maid."

Fortescue was well engrossed in his tale by now, however, and wasn't about to be diverted. "Thought I was a goner, by George. There it was, creeping toward me, damn muzzle on the ground and eyes clamped on me like a ruddy leopard in heat. I knew if I moved I'd end up as his next meal. I could almost feel his blasted fangs sinking into me, tearing my flesh . . . limb to limb."

Cecily watched Doris approach, slowed down by the considerable weight of the tray. Any minute now and she could attract the girl's attention.

"What did I do, you ask?" the colonel suddenly shouted, making Cecily jump. Especially since she'd asked no such thing.

"I really can't imagine," she said faintly.

"I'll tell you what I did, by George! I opened my mouth, and I let out the most blood-curdling roar I could manage." Fortescue then opened his mouth wide.

Cecily could only describe the noise that came out of it as fiendish. The awful sound seemed to vibrate the banisters and rattle the crystal globes of the chandelier. It rose from a bellow and slowly reached the ear-splitting crescendo of a wild scream.

It was too much for Doris. With a shrill shriek she dropped the tray and clapped her hands over her ears. The silver fell with a deafening clatter, then skidded and slid across the polished floor at the edge of the carpet until it finally crashed against the wall. Meanwhile, Doris hopped up and down, wailing at the top of her voice.

For a second or two the colonel stared at her, then with a bellow of fright, took off at a lumbering run down the hallway shouting, "Ambush! Run for your blasted lives, you blithering idiots!"

Cecily rushed over to Doris, just as Baxter's voice echoed from down the hallway. "What in the blue blazes is going on here?"

Doris stood shivering, her hands still over her ears, wailing, "Oh, mum, I'm sorry, I really am, I just couldn't stand it, mum, it was such an awful noise—"

Gently Cecily pulled the girl's hands away from her ears. "It's all right, Doris, don't worry, I'll help you pick up the mess."

"Oh, no, mum, I couldn't let you do that. I'll pick them up. Oh, my, now they'll all have to be washed again. Mrs. Chubb will have my hide for this . . ." She began to sob as she frantically gathered up knives and forks and threw them back onto the tray.

"What on earth—?" Baxter demanded from directly behind Cecily.

She turned, warning him with a finger at her lips. "It's all right, Baxter. The colonel got a little carried away and frightened Doris. She's fine now."

"That lunatic should be locked away," Baxter muttered. "He's going to be the death of someone one of these days."

"He meant no harm." Hearing the front door open, Cecily looked up to see Ned walking into the lobby. The sunlight followed him in, and she couldn't see his face until he'd shut the door.

Then he turned to her, and she knew at once that something was dreadfully wrong. "Ned?" she said tentatively as he came slowly toward her.

Ned's face looked unnaturally pale as he glanced at Baxter. "I'm glad you're here, guv," he said, his voice trembling. "I'm afraid I have terrible news."

Cecily felt an intense urge to reach for Baxter's hand. Curbing the impulse, she demanded sharply, "What's the matter, Ned?"

Ned twisted his cap around and around in his restless fingers. "It's John Thimble, mum. I'm sorry . . . but I'm afraid he's dead."

Cecily heard the words, but they seemed to make no sense. John couldn't possibly be dead. There had to be some dreadful mistake. She stared at Ned, willing him to tell her that it was a macabre joke.

"I'm really sorry, mum," Ned whispered.

Vaguely Cecily heard Baxter's crisp, deep voice. It seemed to be coming from a long, long way off. "What happened?"

Ned's voice sounded even fainter. "I don't know, guv. Looks like he had an accident of some kind. Stuck his shears clean through his neck, 'e did."

Cecily closed her eyes as the floor slowly tilted up to meet her.

"He was so masterful," Doris told an avidly attentive audience in the kitchen later. "He just swept her up in his arms and carried her off down the hallway, yelling at the top of his voice for Ned to fetch the doctor."

Ethel rolled her eyes to the ceiling and clasped her hands to her bosom. "Oo 'eck, how romantic!"

"Where'd he take her?" Gertie demanded, while Mrs.

Chubb just stood there clicking her tongue and shaking her head.

Doris shrugged. "I dunno, do I. Maybe he was taking her to the library."

"Or to his room," Gertie said, giving Ethel a nudge with her elbow.

"Oo 'eck," Ethel said again.

"That's enough, girls," Mrs. Chubb said sharply. "We all have better things to do than to stand around here gossiping about Madam and Mr. Baxter. Ethel, get these potatoes scrubbed. Doris, get busy washing the silverware again. You'll have to help her, Gertie, or the tables won't be ready for the midday meal."

"What about the bleeding dusting, then?" Gertie demanded. "How the bloody hell am I going to do that if I'm down here helping with the flipping washing up?"

Mrs. Chubb whirled on her, breathing fire. "Just do what you're told, Gertie Brown! There's enough trouble going on around here, what with Lord Sittingdon dying, and now poor John Thimble—" Her voice broke, and Doris felt ill as she watched the housekeeper rush from the kitchen, her apron held over her face.

"I never seen Mrs. Chubb upset like that before," she said, her own lip trembling.

Gertie shrugged, though her face looked pale and her eyes looked too bright as she turned away. "She'll get over it," she muttered.

"It must have been an awful sight," Ethel said as she dragged the sack of potatoes across the floor. "Poor old bugger. Wonder how he did it?"

"Ned says as how the shears were sticking out of his neck," Doris said, feeling sick again at the memory of Ned's hushed voice. "Ned reckons he fell on them. Lying there in the middle of the hydrangea bushes he were. One of the guests saw him while she was out walking in the gardens. She rushed back to tell Ned."

"Must have been a shock for her," Ethel said, speaking

louder to be heard above the rumble of potatoes falling into the washtub. "Who was it, do you know?"

"Ned never said." Doris lifted the heavy cauldron from the stove and staggered back with it to the sink. She almost choked in the cloud of steam that arose as she poured the water over the silverware in the sink.

"I wonder if Madam will be all right." Ethel picked up a potato and sliced the end off it.

"'Course she will," Gertie said, plunging her hands into the hot water. "She's got Mr. Baxter taking care of her, ain't she. I bet she's bleeding glad he's back for good."

"Wonder what made him come back here from London. Must have not liked it, I reckon. Just like me and Joe. We couldn't stand it up in the Smoke neither."

Gertie's voice dropped to a low whisper. "I heard that he's bought half of the hotel, so now he's half owner."

"Where'd you hear that?" Ethel demanded.

Gertie lifted a bundle of forks from the water and laid them on the draining board. "Mrs. Chubb got it from Mrs. Carter-Holmes. Ran into her in the hallway upstairs, she did. You know how them two gossip when they get together. Mind you, I think there's more going on than that."

Ethel's eyes grew wide with anticipation. "Watcha mean?"

Gertie shrugged. "I seen the way they bleeding looks at each other, that's all."

"Go on," Ethel said, her voice rising in excitement, "you think he fancies her, then?"

"Course he bleeding fancies her. I've always known that." Gertie fished around for more forks. "It's just that it seems bleeding different now, somehow."

"Do you think he'll ask her to marry him?" Doris asked, her heart beating faster at the thought.

Gertie laughed. "What, Mr. Baxter marry Madam? He'd never have the bleeding guts to ask her."

Ethel sighed. "It would be nice for her, though, wouldn't it? Really romantic."

"Wouldn't be bleeding nice for us, though, would it?" Gertie dropped more forks on the tray as Doris feverishly polished the one in her hand.

"Why not?"

" 'Cos then Mr. Baxter would own all of the bloody Pennyfoot, wouldn't he? Men don't share with wives. We'd all be working for him. That's if he bleeding kept us on, that is." She looked over her shoulder at Ethel. "He's not like Madam, you know. He watches the farthings a lot closer than she does. He might decide they can't afford to keep us all on here. Especially in the winter."

"Oo 'eck," Ethel said gloomily. "I'd have to go back to helping Joe on the farm."

"What would happen to me and Daisy, then?" Doris said fearfully.

"Never mind you and Daisy." Gertie slapped a bunch of knives down on the draining board. "What would happen to me and the babies, that's what I want to know? How would I clothe and feed two little nippers if I'm out on the street?"

The girls fell silent, each absorbed in their own worries. Doris rubbed at the fork until it gleamed, then laid it on the tray with the others. It looked as if she'd have to see about that singing career sooner than she thought.

Now that she was faced with the prospect, it seemed more scary than exciting. For the first time, she was beginning to realize just how hard it would be to be out on her own. It was a scary thought.

"I have fainted once or twice in my life before," Cecily declared, "and I have managed to survive the experience. So please stop fussing over me as if I were about to expire at any moment."

Kevin Prestwick removed his fingers from her wrist and gave her a stern look. "Your temper is an indication that you are out of sorts."

"I am upset, that is all." Cecily looked over at Baxter,

who stood by the French windows. She had recovered from her embarrassing collapse in the lobby and now sat in a chair by the fireplace.

He'd told her that he'd carried her there from the lobby, where apparently she'd fainted. Then he'd held her while she'd cried over the death of John Thimble.

She had never loved him more than she had in those tender moments.

"You have had a nasty shock, Cecily," Prestwick was saying. "I must insist that you take things quietly and rest for the remainder of the day."

"I feel perfectly all right, though I must admit I have a rather beastly headache." Cecily drew her fingers across her forehead. "I just can't believe that John is no longer with us. The Pennyfoot will never be the same again."

"It was a most unusual and extremely unfortunate accident."

She looked up at him, searching his face. "You are quite sure it was an accident?"

Prestwick looked down at her with a quizzical expression. "You have reason to think otherwise?"

"No, of course not," she said hastily. "I just don't understand how it could have happened."

"It was one of those bizarre accidents that happens now and then." The doctor opened his black bag and peered inside. "Apparently your gardener tripped while pruning the shrubs. Instead of letting go of the shears, he instinctively held onto them. The blades were opened, and one of them sliced the jugular vein."

He shook his head and reached inside his bag. "It is indeed strange the manner in which fate works for each of us. The unfortunate man could have fallen a thousand times and not hurt himself. Though a fall is always considerably more dangerous, of course, when one is carrying a lethal instrument."

He withdrew some small envelopes from his bag. "I will

leave these powders with you, Cecily. I want you to take one now, in a glass of water, and another in about six hours. If you still have the headache, you may take another one when you retire for the night. If you are not feeling better in the morning, please consult me again.''

He shut the bag with a snap and turned to look at Baxter. ''I would suggest that you see she gets sufficient rest if you want to see her fully recovered. Severe shock can sometimes have unpleasant delayed effects.''

''I'll do what I can,'' Baxter said, giving Cecily one of his stern looks. ''Mrs. Sinclair has a mind of her own, however. I hope she has the sense to take heed of your warning.''

''Piffle,'' Cecily said rudely. ''I know when I'm feeling all right.''

''Obviously, the sooner you are alone, Madam, the faster you will recover,'' Baxter said pointedly.

Prestwick gave him a look of pure disdain. ''I think that is an excellent idea.'' He inclined his head in a mock bow, then, with a muttered, ''Good day to you both,'' he left the room.

CHAPTER

❀ 10 ❀

"Thank you, Baxter," Cecily said, wishing her head would stop swimming. "All that fussing over me was beginning to get on my nerves."

He came forward, anxiety etched on his face. "How are you feeling, dear Madam, in all honesty?"

Cecily sighed. "In all honesty, Baxter, while I'm saddened and shocked at the death of a very dear friend, I am otherwise in perfect health. Perhaps a twinge of the rheumatics now and again, but nothing more serious than that, I assure you."

Baxter, to her great pleasure, reached for her hand and pressed it to his breast. "If anything should happen to you, Cecily, I should be desolate."

Immeasurably warmed by his words, Cecily smiled up at him. "Have no fear, Baxter. I have every intention of outliving you."

"I shall hold you to that promise." He moved away, taking some of the warmth with him.

Cecily shivered. "They have taken John's body away?"

"Yes, Prestwick has already taken care of it. I didn't want the poor man lying around in full view of everyone."

"No, of course not." She was silent for a moment, dwelling on her uneasy thoughts. "I really have trouble believing that John could be so careless," she said at last. "He has always been so very cautious with his gardening tools."

"He didn't expect to fall, Cecily. That is something one cannot foresee."

"Perhaps, but wouldn't you think that a man who is overly cautious would have the instinct to drop the shears, rather than hold onto them?"

Baxter looked worried. "John Thimble was an old man. One's instincts do not function as swiftly with age. Neither is one as agile. This news is distressing enough. Please don't upset yourself any further with fruitless conjecture."

He was right, of course. There was absolutely no reason why she should suspect anything more serious than an accident—except for the fact that John had kept watch over his precious hydrangeas last night, and she herself had warned him to be careful.

Surely, though, pranksters from the village would not have carried their mischief so far? It seemed unlikely. On the other hand, two deaths in the hotel, within a day of each other, seemed a little bit too much of a coincidence.

She was reluctant to mention her troubled thoughts to Baxter, however. She knew quite well what he would say. He would no doubt insist on informing P. C. Northcott about her suspicions. So far she had been fortunate that he hadn't done so with regard to Michel's possible involvement in Lord Sittingdon's death.

She would have to keep her thoughts to herself, at least until she'd had a chance to investigate further. And, she promised herself, if there was the slightest proof that John's death was not an accident, then she would inform the constable herself. She could only hope and pray that would not become necessary.

It was some time later when she could finally escape from Baxter's diligent eye. He had retired to the office to work on the bookkeeping and had left strict instructions that she stay in the library and pass the time with a book.

He had even gone so far as to pick one out for her, one of her favorite Sherlock Holmes novels. She could not concentrate on it, however, and less than half an hour after Baxter had left her alone, she put the book down and went in search of Michel.

As she expected, she found him in the kitchen, preparing the pheasants for the midday meal. Telling him she wished to discuss the week's menu, she suggested they step outside into the courtyard behind the kitchen, where they could escape from the noise.

After giving him a few suggestions of dishes she would like prepared, she decided to come straight to the point. ''Michel, I want to know exactly what you placed on the tray for Lord Sittingdon the night before last.''

Michel's expression grew instantly guarded. ''I sent him up dinner, *madame.* Ze turtle soup, ze lobster salad, ze trout almandine with lamb cutlets, and . . .'' He circled his hand in the air with a flourish, ''. . . *la piece de resistance,* Grand Marnier souffle. *Voila!*''

''And that is all?'' Cecily inquired.

Michel narrowed his eyes. ''I didn't poison him, if that's what you're thinking,'' he said, forgetting his French accent for the moment. ''I''ll swear to that on me mother's grave. So help me, God. He ate what everybody else in the hotel ate, and nothing else.''

''What about seasonings?'' Cecily said, hating the necessity for this interrogation. ''Perhaps you used something on the gentleman's dinner that might have been tainted?''

''Nothing, mum, I swear.'' Michel held up his hand. ''I used what I always use, the mixture of herbs and seasonings that Madeline Pengrath supplies us with, and that's all. I put exactly the same food on both plates, so help me. They both came back scraped clean as if they'd been washed.''

Cecily nodded. ''Thank you, Michel. I'm sorry for the questions, but if Lady Katherine presses charges, we will have to answer them in court. I just wanted to be sure.''

Michel's face turned white. ''I won't have to go to court, will I? They could put me away for keeps.''

Cecily frowned. ''Michel, I don't wish to pry into your private life, but if you are in trouble, perhaps you should tell me about it. We might be able to help.''

Michel shook his head. ''It's not now, mum, it's what happened in the past. When I was a kid. I got into some bad company, like . . . stealing stuff.''

He hung his head, tracing a pattern in the dust with his shoe. ''I should have known better,'' he muttered.

''People are not imprisoned for life for stealing,'' Cecily said gently.

''That weren't all.'' Michel looked up, and Cecily was shocked at the desperation on his face. ''Swear you won't tell no one, mum. I never told no one . . . it was an accident, on me life. I was opening the nob's safe in the bedroom when he came home and caught me. I went through the window, and he tried to follow me. I made it into the tree outside . . . the bloke didn't. He fell and broke his neck.''

''Oh, Michel,'' Cecily whispered.

The chef looked as if he were about to cry. ''The judge wouldn't listen to me. He said as how I deliberately shoved him out the window. He was going to hang me, mum. That weren't fair. All I did was steal a few things. I didn't deserve to die for that.''

Shaken as she was by this confession, Cecily had to agree with him. ''What happened?''

Michel shrugged. ''I escaped, didn't I? A crowd of us broke out. Some of us made it, some didn't. I heard that the judge swore to get us all, and we'd all hang.''

Cecily briefly closed her eyes. So that was what Michel

had meant by "put away." It was worse than she'd thought. "I assume that Lord Sittingdon was that judge?"

"Yes, mum." Michel's eyes grew fierce. "I didn't do His Lordship in, mum. I swear. But I can't go to court. They'd never believe me. Not after what happened before."

Again she felt compelled to agree with him. She wasn't comfortable about harboring an escaped prisoner, and no doubt the matter would have to be addressed eventually, but this was not the time.

"I'll do my best to see you don't have to appear, and that's all I can promise," she told him. She left him standing alone in the courtyard, and wished she hadn't been responsible for that stricken look on his face.

Knowing her chef as well as she did, she believed what he'd told her. But it wasn't up to her. If she couldn't persuade Lady Katherine not to press charges, then it was likely Michel would be forced to go into court.

Even if no one could prove that he'd poisoned the food, the fact would remain that the hotel would be found at fault. Michel would be under suspicion, and his past would no doubt catch up with him. She could only hope that his misdeeds remained hidden for the time being at least, or he could very well destroy them all.

"I do think that we are out of the woods as far as anyone else being poisoned," Cecily said when Baxter had returned to find her sitting where he'd left her. "Surely if the other guests had eaten tainted food, we would have heard about it by now."

"I agree." Baxter joined her by the fireplace, his serious expression giving her cause for concern. "In that case, however, the question is raised as to why Lord Sittingdon happened to be the only one affected, supposing that everyone ate the same food that night."

Cecily nodded. "It is a mystery, I must admit. Michel swears that the meal he put on the trays was the same food that went into the dining room, and I believe him.

Therefore, I can only assume that something was added to the food in between the time it left the kitchen and the time it arrived at the Sittingdons' suite.''

Noticing Baxter's narrowed eyes, she caught her breath. ''When did you happen to speak to Michel?'' he asked, his voice dangerously quiet.

''This morning.'' She gave him a bright smile.

''When this morning, may I ask? I was under the impression that you had just left your suite when you received the unfortunate news about John's accident.''

''I had.'' She lifted her chin. ''I paid a quick visit below stairs, however, to have a word with Michel while you were in the office. I wasn't aware that I was under orders to remain where I was.''

He gave her the glimmer of a smile. ''I was only considering the doctor's instructions when I asked you to rest. I was concerned for your well-being. I would not presume to issue orders otherwise.''

''I know. I do appreciate your concern, Baxter. I have to admit it is nice to have someone worrying about my welfare again.''

''I have always worried about your welfare, often to my detriment. More often than not, you reviewed my anxiety as interference.''

She closed the book on her lap and laid it on the arm of her chair. ''Only when you tried to prevent me from doing something I felt strongly about.''

''Which usually meant that you were heading into some kind of trouble.''

She sighed. ''Dear Baxter. Tell me, why do you put up with me?''

''Because I care very deeply what happens to you.''

She gazed at him for several moments, then said quietly, ''I trust you know how much I care for you.''

''I do, indeed.''

''Then you will understand when I say that although I will always do my best to please you, sometimes I shall feel compelled to follow my convictions, even though you might protest.''

The affection in his eyes eased her mind. ''My dear madam, I wouldn't have it any other way.''

She wasn't happy about keeping Michel's confession from Baxter, but nothing would be gained by telling him now. Instead, she changed the subject. ''I don't know what to do about the Harvest Ball. Do you think it would be in bad taste to continue with it, in view of John's death?''

Baxter shook his head. ''The ball is a business proposition. I am quite sure that John would understand.''

''I still can't believe he's gone. I wonder if Madeline has heard the news yet. She was the only person, as far as I'm aware, to whom John would talk. He much preferred plants to people. Which is why he talked to Madeline, of course. I think he was fascinated by her vast knowledge of herbs and wildflowers.''

''I can't imagine why. John lived to grow plants. Miss Pengrath gathers them for her bizarre potions. One would think that John would resent someone treating flowers in that outlandish manner.''

''You have to admit, though, Madeline's potions do seem to be uncommonly effective. In fact—'' She broke off as a thought struck her.

Baxter raised an eyebrow. ''In fact?''

Cecily shook her head. ''I was thinking of her latest visit to the Pennyfoot. She delivered a potion to one of our guests. I must inquire if the remedy was successful.''

''If you want my opinion,'' Baxter said gruffly, ''I'd leave well enough alone where that lady is concerned. One never knows if one might end up with the ears of a donkey or the nose of an elephant.''

Cecily laughed. ''Dear Baxter, you have no need to worry. I should still care for you, even with ears of a donkey and the nose of an elephant.''

She lapsed into silence, thinking about Madeline and the potion she had brought to Bella DelRay. Knowing the nature of the potion, Cecily couldn't help wondering now if the singer had taken her revenge on Lord Sittingdon, and somehow managed to administer an overdose of the abortive brew.

Resolving to have a word with Bella at the very first opportunity, Cecily returned her gaze to Baxter, to find him watching her.

"What are you contriving in that busy mind of yours?" he asked with a glint of suspicion in his eye.

"I was trying to decide on the design of gown I shall wear at the ball," she lied blatantly.

"Ah. For a moment I thought you might be planning to investigate the mysterious circumstances of Lord Sittingdon's death."

She pretended to be shocked. "I sincerely hope that the gentleman's death will be considered an unfortunate accident. I intend to speak with Lady Katherine this afternoon, and I shall certainly embrace that theory. I would be foolish to arouse suspicions otherwise, especially since we have not a shred of proof."

"And John Thimble's death?"

"Dr. Prestwick seems convinced it was an accident also."

"I trust you concur?"

She looked him steadily in the eye. "I concur." *That is, until I learn otherwise,* she added inwardly.

"I think it's a really good plan," Ethel said when Gertie had given her all the details. "When are we going to do it, then?"

Gertie snatched up a pile of dirty dishes and dumped them on the tray. "We'll do it tomorrow night," she said, feeling a rush of excitement at the prospect. "I have the evening off, so that will give us plenty of time."

Ethel looked across the empty dining room toward the door. "What about Doris and Daisy? I thought you were going to ask them, too."

"I already bleeding have, haven't I. Doris will have to switch with one of the other girls, but she wants to come. She's never been inside a pub before."

"What about Daisy? Who is going to look after your twins if she comes?"

Gertie grinned. "I asked Mrs. Chubb, didn't I."

"You didn't."

"I bleeding did. After all, she's their bloody fill-in grandma. She was thrilled to bleeding bits."

"So that'll be four of us, then." Ethel thrust a bunch of soiled serviettes into the laundry bag. "Think that'll be enough?"

"It's going to flipping have to be." Gertie heaved a sigh of pure pleasure. "I can't wait to see all their blinking faces when we march in."

"That's if they let us in," Ethel said soberly. "What will we do if they don't?"

"They can't bloody refuse. We'll march in there together, arm in bloody arm. They'd have to bleeding throw us out, and they wouldn't dare do that. They're all too bloody scared to try that. After all, we're bleeding women, ain't we."

"Well, I hope you're right, that's all," Ethel said, looking worried. "I wouldn't want us to get into real trouble."

" 'Course we're not going to get into bleeding trouble," Gertie said with a good deal more confidence than she felt. "We're doing all this in the name of the Women's Movement. Women all over bloody London are doing it."

"But not in Badgers End," Ethel said.

"Maybe not. But if they want to throw us out, they'd have to call the bleeding constable to do it proper like. Do you know how long it would take P. C. Northcott to get there? Bloody hours. By that time we'll be flipping long gone."

"I don't know what Joe's going to say," Ethel muttered, dragging a stained tablecloth off one of the tables.

Gertie snorted. "Doesn't matter what he bleeding says,

does it? You have a bloody right to stand up for what you flipping believe in. Remember, we women have to stick together in this bleeding fight, or we're not going to win it.''

"You sound like Winnie Atkins," Ethel said, looking nervously around as if she expected someone to pounce on her at any second.

"Do I?" Gertie was delighted. "I think she's bloody wonderful. She gets my flipping blood all stirred up, I can tell you.''

Ethel shoved the tablecloth into the laundry bag and took a clean one off the trolley. "I don't know," she said, shaking her head. "That woman frightens me sometimes.''

Gertie heaved an exasperated sigh. "Go on with you, Ethel. You're scared of any bleeding thing what's different.''

"I don't know as I want to be that different." Ethel shook out the square of linen and laid it across the table. "Here, hand me that cruet set and the serviette rings, please.''

Gertie picked up the small silver tray holding the salt and pepper shakers and vinegar bottle and passed it over. "Everything is going to be bleeding different. It's different now, what with them flipping noisy motorcars everywhere. They've even got bloody machines what can fly now. The whole bloody world is changing, and we've got to blinking change with it.''

Ethel gave her a sly look. "You've been talking to those suffragettes a lot, haven't you?" she said smugly.

"Yes, I have. I think what they're doing is going to help bleeding women everywhere one day. We won't have to do what men tell us to bleeding do no more. We'll be able to do whatever we bloody well like.''

"You do what you like now," Ethel said, arranging the silverware neatly on the table. "You don't have a man telling you what to do.''

"I don't have a bleeding man paying for me babies, either." Gertie balanced a cup inside another one and set them on the tray. "Winnie says as how men should have to bleeding pay for the babies they bring into this world. If they did that, maybe they wouldn't be so bloody quick to have their way whenever they gets the blooming chance."

"Shh," Ethel said, glancing over her shoulder again. "You'll get us both into trouble, talking like that out here. What if somebody heard you?"

"I don't care if someone did blinking hear me." Gertie tossed her head. "I have a right to talk any way I want. The bleeding men do, and no one says nothing to them."

"It isn't proper for a woman to talk about such things in public."

"If it ain't bleeding proper for women, then it ain't bleeding proper for men. That's what the flipping Women's Movement is fighting for."

She gave Ethel a hearty nudge that sent the serviette rings she was holding rolling across the table.

Making a frantic grab for them, Ethel muttered, "Watch it, Gertie. I don't want to have to wash them again."

Ignoring her, Gertie flung her hand out, the way she'd seen Winnie Atkins do on the Esplanade. "We're fighting for women's bleeding rights, and we'll keep on flipping fighting until women are treated as bleeding equals."

"That'll be the day," Ethel muttered as she threaded serviettes through the rings.

Gertie nudged her again. "Cheer up, Ethel. We're going to go down in bleeding history, we are, just like the bloody King of England. Wouldn't you like a bunch of nippers reading about you some day in the history books?"

"Not if it means I got to starve in prison," Ethel said, shuddering.

Gertie clicked her tongue, sounding for a moment like Mrs. Chubb. "Go on, Ethel, you're not going to go to prison. It's not as if we're going to bloody set fire to the bleeding George and Dragon, now is it?''

"I s'pose not." Ethel gathered up the laundry bag and headed for the door. ''Just don't forget to fill up those cruet sets. Mrs. Chubb will have a pink fit if she finds them empty again.''

''I won't forget.'' Gertie leaned across the table to brush the crumbs into her small dustpan. Bleeding toffs spilled more salt on the table than what went down their gullets, she thought crossly. If anything ought to be bloody equal, it should be the blinking toffs and the working people. It wasn't bleeding fair that the toffs should have all the money, and the rest of them nothing.

Straightening her back, she cast a long look around the dining room with its spotless white tablecloths and upholstered rosewood chairs. One day it would be different, she thought wistfully. Maybe not for her, but maybe for her little daughter. Maybe by the time that James and Lilly had grown up, the world would be fairer to women.

That's who she was fighting for really, she told herself as she filled the pepper pots. Not herself, but her Lilly. And that made it all the more important. Now she was looking forward to tomorrow night more than ever.

CHAPTER

❀ 11 ❀

As Gertie carried the heavy tray across the foyer later, she caught sight of Ned by the front door. He winked at her, then looked all around before beckoning to her.

She went reluctantly, still unsure of how she felt about the exuberant young man.

"Whatcha, me old cock sparrer!" Ned said softly as she reached him. "How's your mother off for dripping, then?"

"Me mother's been dead and bleeding gone since I was a little nipper," Gertie said curtly. "I already bloody told you that once."

"All right, all right, keep your bloody hair on. It's only an expression, ain't it." Ned winked at her again. "So how about you and me taking a little stroll in the moonlight on your next evening off, then?"

"Can't. I'm bleeding busy." Gertie turned away, shifting the loaded tray against her hip.

Ned chuckled. "Oh, ho, what's this, then? Got a secret admirer, have we?"

Gertie felt her cheeks growing warm. "None of your bleeding business, Ned 'arris."

"Go on, darlin', you can tell old Ned here. Meeting him in the dark on the beach, I wager."

Stung, Gertie forgot about keeping her plan secret. "If you must know, Mr. Nosy-bleeding-Parker, me and the girls are going to go down to the pub tomorrow night. So there."

Ned narrowed his eyes. "Oh, yeah? Who's taking you, then?"

"No one's bleeding taking us, are they. We're going by our bloody selves." Before she knew it, she was telling him the whole thing.

By the time she was finished, Ned was shaking his head in disbelief. "You're all bloody daft if you think you can make a difference," he said, wagging his finger at her. "You women ain't never going to get tiddlywinks, leave alone the bloody vote. You can't fight the government, luv, and no one knows that better than I do."

"We can if there's bloody enough of us." Gertie lifted her chin. "You wait and see, Ned 'arris. We'll show the bleeding lot of you. You and all them bloody buggers down the George and Dragon. You'll see."

With that she heaved the tray up in her arms and marched to the kitchen steps as though she were marching into the battlefields of the Boer War.

Cecily waited until after the midday meal to visit Bella. Baxter had announced his intention to go into the village that afternoon to run an errand, and that left Cecily with time to conduct a furtive investigation.

Since Bella had not made an appearance in the dining room, Cecily assumed that the singer had taken her meal in her suite. After giving the maids enough time to clear away the trays, Cecily mounted the stairs to Bella's floor.

After tapping several times on the door, she received no answer from within the room. Then she rapped louder and was rewarded with a small sound that could have been a groan.

Concerned now, she knocked harder. "Miss DelRay?" she called out. "This is Mrs. Sinclair. I would like to speak with you about an important matter if I may."

She waited for several seconds before she heard the lock click. Then the door slowly opened. The singer remained behind the door as she said in a weakened voice, "Mrs. Sinclair? I'm sorry, but I'm not feeling very well. Perhaps you can come back later?"

Cecily's heart seemed to stop. Surely the singer hadn't been poisoned? Then she remembered the reason for her visit. Of course Bella DelRay wasn't well, if she was taking Madeline's potion. Though why the woman hadn't waited until she'd returned home to face her ordeal, Cecily couldn't imagine.

"I really think I should talk to you now, Miss DelRay," Cecily said as the door started to close. "Miss Pengrath took me into her confidence. Under the circumstances, you might need some help. I'm here to offer it."

There was a long pause, though the door remained ajar. "Miss Pengrath should not have done that," Bella said in a voice tight with pain. "This was supposed to be highly confidential."

Worried that she might have landed Madeline into trouble, Cecily thought fast. "Miss Pengrath was worried that you would not receive the proper care should something go wrong. She asked me to keep an eye on you. I can assure you that no one else shall know of your condition. I simply want to be certain that you are not in any danger, that's all."

"I am not in danger." Another long pause, and then the door opened wider. "I could do with some company, though. If you have time to spare?"

"Plenty of time," Cecily assured her. She stepped inside

the room and closed the door behind her. Bella stood with
her back toward the door. She wore a long silk kimono,
decorated with quite extraordinary peacocks in gloriously
brilliant colors upon a dark blue background.

It was a magnificent garment, full and flowing, and Cecily fell in love with it instantly. "What a beautiful gown,"
she said, admiring the splendid fabric. "It really is most
unusual."

"I beg your pardon?" Bella turned around to face her.
"Oh, thank you. It was a gift from an admirer."

"A magnificent gift," Cecily said, then caught her breath
at the sight of Bella's face.

There was hardly a vestige of color in the woman's
cheeks, and black shadows ringed her eyes. Her hair, the
color of burnished chestnut, was loosely caught on top of
her head. Strands of it had escaped from the comb, and
hung limply about the singer's drawn features.

Shocked at the change in the artiste since her arrival,
Cecily forgot about her suspicions. Although she found it
difficult to condone the woman's actions, she could well
understand the reasons for them.

All her nurturing instincts rushed to the forefront as she
grasped the singer's arm. "My dear, you look absolutely
dreadful. May I send for Dr. Prestwick? I can assure you,
your secret will be safe with him."

Tight-lipped, Bella shook her head. "Thank you, Mrs.
Sinclair, but I do believe the worst is over. I am already
feeling better than I did earlier."

"It might have been more prudent if you had waited until
you returned home to . . . er . . . use the potion," Cecily
said, feeling somewhat awkward. "Surely you would have
had someone there who could have taken care of you?"

Bella laughed, but it wasn't a pleasant sound. "If I had
gone through this in London, someone would surely have
discovered the cause of my incapacity. Within a few hours,
the entire West End would have known about it. I could
not risk my career that way."

"No, of course not." Cecily coughed delicately. "Has the—is it—?"

Bella nodded. "I took care to bury everything in the gardens. I was on my way back this morning when I saw that poor man lying in the bushes. Such a dreadful shock, coming on top of my ordeal—"

She swayed, and Cecily led her to a chair. Seating herself opposite her, she said quietly, "I hadn't realized that you were the person who found John's body. I had assumed that Ned—"

Bella shook her head. She looked so pale Cecily was afraid the singer would faint dead away in front of her. "I came to get help. I told Ned, and he went back to see what had happened."

Realizing that it must have been Bella she saw early that morning, Cecily patted her arm in sympathy. "How awful for you."

"And for you." Bella raised pink-tinted eyes. "I understand the gardener had been with you a long time."

"Since the hotel opened." Cecily paused, waiting for the desolation to pass. "He will be sorely missed. It will be extremely difficult to replace him."

"May I offer my sympathies?" Bella murmured.

"And I mine. This must have been a difficult decision for you to make."

"On the contrary." Bella sighed. "I knew the moment I was certain that I was with child I should have to be rid of it." Her expression changed, becoming vindictive. With her lack of color and her dark-rimmed eyes, she looked quite evil for a moment. Her voice dropped to a vicious whisper. "May its father be damned in hell."

Realizing that Bella wasn't aware she knew the identity of the baby's father, Cecily decided to keep that to herself. "I'm sure you don't mean that," she said quietly. "You must have cared for the father, or you would not have . . ." She allowed her voice to trail off.

Bella looked up. "Women such as I are rarely fortunate

enough to find someone with whom we can share a loving relationship,'' she said, her voice hard with bitterness. ''Good men do not pursue women who are on the stage. No matter how chaste we might be, we are nevertheless labeled as harlots, simply because of our choice of profession. Rather unjust, wouldn't you say?''

''Undoubtedly,'' Cecily agreed.

''After a while, sheer loneliness drives some of us to live up to our reputation. Hence the belief is vindicated amongst the stage-door Romeos.'' She lifted her chin, closing her eyes for a brief moment before continuing. ''I had accepted an invitation in good faith, anticipating a pleasant interlude and nothing more. Unfortunately my loathsome Lothario expected much more. When I resisted, he became incensed and overpowered me. This was the result.''

''I'm so sorry,'' Cecily murmured, beginning to feel uncomfortable in the face of such honesty.

Bella shrugged. ''Fate has a way of repaying its debts. I can only hope he has suffered as much as I.''

No doubt he had, Cecily thought, watching the singer's face carefully. Had Bella DelRay induced Lord Sittingdon's unpleasant death by her own hand? It was hard to tell from her expression, marred as her face was from her own suffering.

Deciding that she wasn't going to learn much more at this point, Cecily rose from the chair. ''Do, please, send for me if you need any assistance. There is no need to explain to anyone else. If I receive word from you, I shall come alone.''

Bella raised her eyes and gave her a bleak smile. ''I am hoping that I shall recover soon enough to travel back to London. You have been most kind, Mrs. Sinclair. I appreciate your concern, but I assure you I shall be quite all right.''

Cecily left her alone and walked thoughtfully down the hallway to the stairs. Bella certainly had good reason to want Lord Sittingdon to suffer, but enough to kill him? Somehow she didn't think so.

As long as she was on the same floor, she decided, she might as well take this opportunity to talk with Lady Katherine. Aware that the meeting was bound to be unpleasant, she'd been putting off the moment when she would have to face the grieving widow.

Now she had no more excuses, and the sooner she learned the worst, the quicker she could deal with it.

Bracing herself, Cecily approached Lady Katherine's suite and knocked on the door.

''Now we all bleeding know what we're supposed to do, so don't nobody bleeding botch it up,'' Gertie warned the little group cramped around her in the narrow pantry. ''And remember, for Gawd's sake, don't tell the old battle-ax where we're going. She'd wet her bleeding drawers if she knew what we was planning on doing.''

''She's looking after the babies tomorrow night, isn't she?'' Daisy asked anxiously.

Gertie glared at her. '' 'Course she is, silly. But she don't have to bleeding know what we're up to. She'd stop us from going if she did.''

''What about Joe?'' Ethel demanded, shifting away from the sack of garlic under her nose. ''What do I tell him?''

''Tell him you've offered to take someone's place here for the evening. Say that Mrs. Chubb asked you to stay.''

Ethel looked horrified. ''That'd be lying! What if he finds out where I really was? He'd near on kill me, he would.''

Gertie crossed her arms, then swore as her elbow contacted sharply with the bread bin on the shelf next to her. ''You're going to bleeding tell him you're going down the bloody George and Dragon, then?''

Ethel shook her head violently, dislodging her cap. ''No, no, of course not.'' She reached up and pinned the cap more securely.

"Can't you tell him you're going to help Miss Brown do something, without telling him what it is?" Doris suggested timidly.

"Shut up, you bleeding twerp," Gertie said rudely.

"No, wait a minute, that might do the trick." Ethel thought about it a minute. "I could say as how you had a job to do, and it was going to take you all evening, so I offered to help you. That wouldn't exactly be lying, would it?"

" 'Course not," Gertie said, giving Doris a hearty slap on the back that just about shot her into the door. "And if he catches you down the bleeding pub, you can tell him that's where the flipping job was."

"I hope he doesn't catch me," Ethel muttered.

Gertie nodded approvingly at Doris. "Good idea, Doris. Finally using your bleeding bonce for once, aren't you."

"Yes, Miss Brown. Thank you, Miss Brown," Doris murmured doubtfully.

"Anyhow, we all meet outside the stable gate at half past six tomorrow night, then, all right?"

"What if Samuel sees us?" Doris asked nervously. "You know how he's always watching me to see what I do."

Gertie sighed. "I don't know why you don't put that poor bleeding bugger out of his misery. Either tell him you like him, or tell him you hate him. Then he'll stop bleeding hanging around you, won't he. He's going bloody bonkers trying to guess which it is."

Doris's face turned bright red.

"She likes him," Daisy said shortly. "She just doesn't like him enough to tell him, that's all. She'd rather waste her time trying to get on the stage."

Doris lifted her chin and glared at her twin. "It's not a waste of time, so there. Bella DelRay said as how she'd help me when I'm old enough to go, and she knows everyone on the Variety stage."

"She hasn't heard you sing yet," Daisy said, glaring back.

"I know, but I told her what everyone else says about my singing. And I'm going to sing for her before she goes back to London."

"You won't be able to sing anymore if you don't shut up and listen to what I'm saying," Gertie said, losing patience with the twins' constant bickering. "I'll bleeding bash your heads together, so help me I will."

Doris and Daisy fell silent, though their faces still glowered.

Gertie cleared her throat. "We meet at the bleeding stable gate at half past six like I said, all right?"

"All right," everyone hastily chanted in unison.

"And don't bleeding worry yourself over Samuel. He's off at six, so he won't even be there, will he."

Doris looked relieved.

"Well, I've got to get back to the babies," Daisy said, turning for the door. "I've left them alone long enough. They'll be waking up soon, and heaven knows what they'll get into if I'm not there."

Gertie grimaced. "I haven't seen them all day. They'll be forgetting who their bleeding mother is at this rate."

Daisy smiled, something she rarely did. "They're growing up so fast. They'll soon be a year old."

"Yeah, I know." Gertie sighed. "Once they start walking proper, there'll be no bloody holding them."

She jumped as the housekeeper's irate voice rang out from the kitchen. "Gertie! Ethel? Where the devil are you, Doris? What are all these plates doing on the kitchen table, then?"

"Dancing the bleeding jig," Gertie muttered.

"Oo, 'eck," Ethel said, making a dive for the door.

Gertie stopped her, placing a finger over Ethel's lips. "Don't forget, mum's the word. Now bugger off, before the old—"

Mrs. Chubb suddenly appeared in the doorway, eyes

blazing in her flushed face. "What in heaven's name are you all doing in here? Why aren't you in the dining room, Gertie? Daisy? You haven't left those babies alone, have you?"

"I'm just going, Mrs. Chubb, honest." Daisy fled through the door, followed by Doris, who fell over her twin's feet in her haste.

"I'm on me way to the bleeding dining room, ain't I," Gertie said belligerently, meeting the housekeeper's stormy glare. "Cor strewth, I don't get no bloody time to breathe here, that I don't."

She stomped out to the kitchen, leaving Ethel to explain why she was lurking around in the pantry instead of picking the radishes for the dinner salad.

CHAPTER

❀ 12 ❀

Lady Katherine answered Cecily's knock and invited her into the suite. Lord Sittingdon's widow was a tall, delicate-looking woman, whose fading beauty had not been overly marred by the recent tragic events.

Although the dark circles under her eyes were evidence of a sleepless night, she appeared composed as she offered Cecily a seat by the window overlooking the ocean.

"I wish to thank you, Mrs. Sinclair, for seeing to my husband's affairs. Dr. Prestwick assured me last night that Bertram's . . . body . . . would be on the train to London by the end of the week."

"Yes," Cecily said gently. "I understand that members of your family will be meeting the train. I assume that you will wish to leave earlier. I will have Samuel take you to the station."

"No, I—" Lady Katherine lifted a shaky hand and held

her fingers to her eyes. "Forgive me, Mrs. Sinclair. I do not feel well enough to travel. I have decided to stay here and travel back with my husband's . . . body."

Realizing that the widow was not nearly as composed as she appeared, Cecily hastened to reassure her. "But of course. I understand. Your suite has been booked until the end of the week, in any case."

"Thank you." Lady Katherine lowered her hand, revealing tears brimming in her soft blue eyes. "I am sure I shall have recovered enough in a day or two—" Her voice broke.

Cecily drew in a deep breath. "Lady Katherine, I cannot begin to tell you how extremely sorry I am about the unfortunate circumstances of your husband's death. The entire staff of the Pennyfoot Hotel joins with me in extending their deepest sympathy."

"You are all very kind," Lady Katherine murmured, wiping away a tear.

Selecting her words carefully, Cecily went on. "I realize that the cause of Lord Sittingdon's death will have to be investigated. If it is found that the hotel is responsible, I assure you—"

"Mrs. Sinclair." The widow lifted her face and gave Cecily a direct look. "I have given this matter some considerable thought."

Cecily held her breath, waiting in an agonizing silence as Lady Katherine discreetly blew her nose on her fine lawn handkerchief. Then the widow breathed a deep sigh.

"There will be no charges leveled against this hotel, Mrs. Sinclair. I wish to put your mind at rest about that. My husband's death was an unfortunate and tragic accident. No matter what the results of the postmortem reveal, I do not wish to be embroiled in a lengthy investigation. It would be too upsetting. I simply want to take my dear husband's body home and bury him in peace."

Her voice caught on a sob, and Cecily waited in silence for the widow to compose herself again. "Forgive me," she murmured at last. "I'm finding this most difficult."

"Lady Katherine," Cecily said quietly, "I need hardly say how grateful I am—"

"Please." The widow raised her hand. "The matter is settled." Her hand fell in her lap as she sighed. "I still cannot believe Bertram is gone."

She looked up, her eyes filled with sorrow. "He wasn't feeling well soon after we arrived, you know, which was why we ordered the evening meal in our suite. When the tray arrived, my husband said he wasn't hungry, but I urged him to eat something. I thought at the time that the lobster didn't taste very good. As a matter of fact, I didn't eat my salad. I sent it back to the kitchen."

She gave Cecily a wan smile. "Lobster salad is one of my favorite dishes, you know. It was fortunate that I didn't eat it that night, however, or I might be lying dead next to poor Bertram. Had I not insisted on him eating his meal, he would have been alive today."

Tears spilled out of her eyes and down her cheeks, and she sought for her handkerchief once more. "I really don't know how I shall manage without him," she sobbed, her voice muffled by the handkerchief. "How I wish I had never suggested coming down here to celebrate our wedding anniversary. Now I shall always remember it as the terrible day my beloved Bertram passed away." She pressed her handkerchief to her mouth as if to prevent the sobs.

Cecily rose, wishing she could find the words of comfort that were always so elusive at times like this. "I am so sorry, Lady Katherine. Can I get you anything?"

Lady Katherine shook her head. She turned her gaze to the window, and folded her hands in her lap. "It was so sudden," she whispered, barely loud enough for Cecily to hear. "He was such a good man. He didn't deserve to die that way."

Cecily's thoughts flew to the suffragettes. There were at least two women who thought he had deserved to die.

She left the widow still gazing out of the window, and made her way down the stairs. Baxter would be pleased to hear that the hotel would not be held responsible for the death of Lord Sittingdon. Now that the danger of that had passed, she could relax a little.

John Thimble's funeral had been set for Friday. She must make sure that those who wished to attend were free to go. She also had to see about hiring another gardener, though the thought of that depressed her no end.

There would never be another gardener like John. One only had to explore the grounds of the Pennyfoot to know how very much he had loved his work. The rose garden, John's pride and joy, had been so lovingly tended and zealously guarded against pests, whether of the insect variety or otherwise.

The rolling lawns, the grass tennis courts, and the bowling greens had always looked like lush green carpets, and the topiaries were as neatly trimmed as Colonel Fortescue's beard.

Where, Cecily wondered, was she going to find someone else who cared enough to maintain the pristine quality of the Pennyfoot gardens? The task seemed as impossible as unearthing the truth about Lord Sittingdon's death.

It was almost an hour later before Gertie could speak with Ethel again. She was actually on her way out of the dining room when Ethel came rushing in with the clean serviettes.

"That Mrs. Chubb is as angry as an irritated wasp over something," she muttered as she flew past Gertie. "No one can do anything right, not even Michel."

"Wait a minute," Gertie said urgently, "I've been thinking. I think we should tell Winnie Atkins what we plan to do tomorrow night."

Ethel stopped short, her mouth dropping open. "Why? I thought it was supposed to be a secret."

"Well, it is, but we have to tell her and Muriel. What if they want to come with us?"

Ethel's eyes widened. "Oo, 'eck, you really think they would?"

Gertie shrugged. "I dunno, do I. But it would make bleeding more of us if they did, wouldn't it?"

"Yeah, it would." Ethel's face lit up. "And Winnie would know how to do things proper, since she's done it before so many times."

Gertie took offense at that. "I know how to bleeding do it proper," she said, bristling with resentment. "I could bloody well do it without them easy enough. It's just that the more flipping women we have with us, the better."

"So let's ask them, then." Ethel threaded the serviettes into the rings and darted to the next table.

"All right, but it will have to be first thing in the morning. I'll help you take the hot water jugs up, then we'll have time to talk to them."

Ethel stopped short, her face creased in a frown. "What about the stove? You won't have time to clean it if you help me with the hot water."

"Don't bleeding worry about that. I'll take care of it later."

Ethel half-heartedly nodded her agreement, and Gertie left the dining room well pleased with herself.

She could barely contain her excitement at the thought of what she had planned and hardly slept throughout the night, trying not to wake the babies as she tossed around on her narrow bed.

For as long as she could remember, she'd resented the way she'd been treated by the men in her life. First her father, who'd beaten her senseless at times, and then Ian, who'd taught her how to love and then betrayed her. She'd married him, only to find out he was already married. But by then the twins were on the way, and she'd had to accept the depressing fact that she was on her own.

Ross McBride had entered her life only briefly, but he had left a lasting impression. Maybe if she hadn't been so badly mistreated, she told herself, she might have trusted him enough to forget her fears. But experience had taught her bleeding well.

Men wanted women for what they could get out of them, and nothing more. It was time they learned that women had feelings, too, as well as brains. There were a lot more things that women could do besides cooking, cleaning, and lying on their backs whenever their man felt bleeding amorous.

Gertie smiled in the darkness, remembering the woman doctor who had stayed at the Pennyfoot. It was before she'd married Ian, and the doctor had taught her a thing or two about what went on between a man and a woman. She'd really liked that doctor. If things had been different, she might have ended up being a doctor herself.

Gertie turned her head toward her sleeping babies. She couldn't see them in the darkness, but she could hear their breathing. James was more than likely lying on his back. She could hear him snuffling in his sleep. Lilly always lay curled up on her side, one small fist tucked under her chin.

It was Lilly who would have to fight for what she wanted in her life, Gertie thought, feeling a strange ache around her heart. The world was changing so bleeding fast, but would things change fast enough to give her daughter the chances her mother never had?

She could only flipping hope they would. And if she could do one tiny thing to help those changes come about, she'd bloody do it. For Lilly, and for every other sleeping little girl out there. Hugging her excitement to herself, she made a determined effort to sleep.

It was still dark when she met Ethel in the kitchen the next morning. Together they lifted the steaming cauldrons of water from the stove and carefully filled the first of the china jugs to the top. Then they trudged up and down the stairs, delivering the cumbersome jugs to each of the bedrooms.

They left the sleeping suffragettes' floor until last, winding up in front of the suite just as dawn was breaking. Gertie was just about to lift a hand to give a firm rap on the door when the sound of muffled voices suddenly erupted from inside the room.

Gertie soon realized that the two friends inside were arguing with each other. The words were too low to be distinguished, but every now and then a voice was raised in anger, and occasionally a slap of something being slammed down accompanied the tirade.

Gertie recognized Winnie's strident voice, overriding Muriel's higher-pitched tones. Slowly she dropped her hand and looked at Ethel. "Blimey," she whispered, "they aren't half bleeding going at it. Maybe we better not ask them right now. Let's just give them the water jugs and hop it."

Ethel nodded, her face creased with anxiety. "Can't we just leave the jugs outside?" she whispered back.

" 'Course not." Gertie lifted her hand again, but then Winnie's voice rang out from close behind the door. She was apparently on the point of leaving, and now her words were crystal clear.

"I'm well aware that we went too far, but it's too late to do anything about it now, isn't it. Don't forget, you are as much involved in this as I am, so you'd better be careful what you say. We could both very well end up in jail for the rest of our lives this time. You'd do well to remember that."

The door opened abruptly, and Winnie stood frozen to the spot, her face draining of color when she saw Ethel and Gertie standing in front of her.

"We just brought the water jugs, Miss Atkins," Ethel said nervously. She thrust the jug into Winnie's unresisting hands, then without another word, turned and fled down the corridor. Winnie watched her go, then turned her cold gaze on Gertie. Speechless for once, Gertie handed her the other jug. Winnie took it from her, then promptly slammed the door in Gertie's face.

Catching up with Ethel on the stairs, Gertie said breathlessly, "I wonder what the bleeding hell they've been up to."

"I dunno," Ethel said, practically running down the steps, "and I don't think I want to know."

They both practically tumbled into the lobby, much to the surprise of Cecily, who was on her way to the kitchen to have a word with Gertie.

Looking at their flushed faces, she wondered what it was that had unsettled the two young women so. She refrained from asking, however, since the housemaids' affairs was Mrs. Chubb's domain, and the housekeeper would not thank her for interfering in her business.

Instead, she bade the two breathless girls a cheerful, "Good morning!"

"Morning, mum." They'd spoken together and glanced at each other, as if sharing a dire secret.

Cecily envied their close communication. Madeline was perhaps the only woman with whom she shared that kind of relationship, and she saw her so rarely. She would have to make an effort to spend more time with her friend, she thought.

Realizing that the two housemaids were staring at her expectantly, she gave herself a mental shake. "I understand that you took the tray up to Lord Sittingdon's suite the other night, Gertie."

Gertie shoved her apron strap back onto her shoulder. "Yes, that's right, I did, mum. I took it up and brought it back again later."

"I see." Cecily paused, wondering how best to phrase the question. There didn't seem to be any way except to ask outright. "Did you happen to meet anyone while on the way up there?"

Gertie looked surprised. "Only them suffragettes, mum. They met me on the landing." She frowned, sending a nervous glance at Ethel as if for reassurance. "Did I do something wrong?"

"No, Gertie, of course not." Cecily smiled at their worried faces. "I was just wondering if you had taken trays to any of the other rooms that night, that's all."

"Oh." Gertie looked relieved. "No, I didn't, mum. I don't know if someone else might have, though. I know that Miss Atkins and Miss Croft ate their dinners in the dining room 'cos they told me. I don't think they could have ate very much, though."

Cecily looked at her closely. "What makes you say that, Gertie?"

"Well, mum, when I asked them if I could get them something, they said they wanted the bl— I mean, the tray I was holding. Well, it were the tray for Lord Sittingdon's suite, weren't it, so I said as how they couldn't have that one, but I'd bring them up another one."

Cecily nodded. "What did they say to that?"

Gertie screwed up her face in her effort to remember. "Well, Miss Croft started to say something about Lord Sittingdon, but then Miss Atkins laughed, really loud, and said they'd already eaten their dinner. They both started talking at once, then. You know, like people do sometimes and you don't know which one to look at? Anyway, there I was, wasn't I, turning back and forth to both of them until I tell you, mum, I was getting bleeding dizzy."

Ethel gasped at Gertie's lapse, but Cecily pretended not to notice the cursing. "What were they talking about, can you remember?"

Gertie shrugged. "I dunno, mum. Couldn't blinking understand it all, they was talking so blinking fast. I think they was having a bloody game with me, that's what."

"Gertie!" Ethel whispered loudly, nudging her with her elbow.

Gertie glared at her. "What!"

"Your language," Ethel muttered.

Gertie had the grace to look repentant. "Sorry, mum. It sort of bloody slips out now and again."

"So I've noticed." Cecily glanced at the grandfather clock in the corner. The Westminster chimes were about to announce the breakfast hour. She'd promised to meet Baxter in the dining room for breakfast, and he hated to be kept waiting. ''That will be all, then, Gertie, thank you. You had best get back to the kitchen now.''

Gertie nodded. ''Yes, mum. Thank you, mum.'' She dropped an awkward curtsey, waited for Ethel to bob hers, then the two of them dashed off across the lobby with their skirts flying, in what Mrs. Chubb would have described as a deplorably unladylike manner.

Feeling decidedly uneasy, Cecily hurried down the hallway toward the dining room. She kept picturing Winnie Atkins and Muriel Croft, talking earnestly to Gertie, making her turn this way and that with the loaded tray in her hands.

Could it be possible that one of them had distracted Gertie enough, offering the other the chance to sprinkle something over the food? It seemed highly unlikely. Then again, she might not have heard the entire story from Gertie.

Sighing, Cecily reached the door of the dining room, her glance traveling to the far corner where her table was situated. Baxter was already there, a newspaper propped up against the teapot in front of him.

She couldn't imagine why she was still pursuing the theory that someone had deliberately poisoned Lord Sittingdon. Except that several people here in the hotel had reason to despise the arrogant aristocrat.

There was also Baxter's comment that since no one else appeared to have ingested the poison, it would seem that the aristocrat was the intended victim of a devious act.

Whether or not his actual death was intended, or perhaps a result of a dangerous prank taken too far, Cecily could only guess. The fact remained that if one of her guests had been struck down intentionally by the hand of another, it was her duty to discover the facts and expose the culprit.

Winnie Atkins and Muriel Croft were two high-spirited, strong-willed, rebellious women who had been badly mistreated by the dead man. It would appear that they had ample cause to want to see him suffer.

Making up her mind to question the two women at the earliest opportunity, Cecily placed a determined smile on her face and prepared to enjoy the next hour or two in the company of the man she dearly loved.

CHAPTER

❀ 13 ❀

Baxter greeted Cecily warmly as she approached, though he discreetly refrained from touching her as he waited for her to be seated, no doubt conscious of the scattering of guests seated in the dining room.

"You are looking a little strained this morning," he commented once they were settled. "Are you still not feeling well? I was hoping a night's sleep might improve your health."

"I am quite well, thank you, Baxter." She smiled a little wanly at him. "I'm afraid I didn't sleep too well, that's all. My mind won't let me rest."

Baxter frowned, studying her face. "What particular problem is keeping you awake at night, may I ask?"

Cecily paused as Doris reached the table and set a steaming bowl of porridge in front of her. She placed another bowl in front of Baxter, then stood back. "Shall I bring a fresh pot of tea, mum?" she asked.

"Please, if you will, Doris." Cecily waited until she had scurried off, then said lightly, "There are many issues on my mind at present. All of them demanding my attention."

"That's why I'm here, to help lighten the load if I can."

"I know, Baxter," she said, reassuring him with her smile. "And I hope you are aware of how very much I appreciate and enjoy you being here. Without you I should have a great deal more to worry about than I do now."

He seemed not at all appeased by her words. "Is it only this business of Lord Sittingdon that has you upset, or is there something else troubling you? If so, I should like to know, so that I might attempt to ease your mind. I sincerely hope that you are not having second thoughts about our partnership?"

Dear Baxter, she thought, wishing she could touch his face. "Of course I am not having second thoughts." Glancing across the room, she saw Doris approaching with the teapot. She waited once more for the maid to leave before adding, "As a matter of fact, it was John Thimble who occupied my mind last night. I keep thinking about him lying there in the bushes all alone. I can't help wondering if he died instantly or lay there in pain, waiting in vain for help."

"My dear madam." Baxter reached for her hand and patted it. "You must stop tormenting yourself with such nightmares. I'm quite sure that John would have died on the spot, as he fell."

Perhaps, Cecily thought. But now that she had raised the question, it would haunt her unless she had the answer. There was only one person who could give her that answer. She would have to pay a visit to Dr. Prestwick that afternoon.

Baxter, of course, would be most put out by that. Perhaps it would be better if she refrained from telling him of her intention. She would mention it to him later, after she had returned. He would still be upset, no doubt, but it would be too late for him to prevent her from visiting the doctor.

She poured the hot tea into the china cups, deploring the necessity to keep things from him. If only he were more flexible about such things, she thought crossly, she wouldn't be put into this uncomfortable position.

"Is there nothing I can say that will take that frown from your face?"

She looked up with a start. "I'm sorry, Baxter. I don't mean to depress you with my sorry mood. I just find it hard to believe that I shall not be seeing John again. I was talking to him just two days ago about—" She broke off, suddenly remembering the entire conversation.

"About what?" Baxter prompted, watching her curiously.

"About the hydrangeas," she said slowly. "He was talking about pruning them." He had also talked about the village youths, she added inwardly. The young men whom he suspected had been chopping off the blossoms.

She had warned him to be careful, worried that the boisterous lads might not consider John's frailty and act roughly with him, especially if he attempted to defend his precious flowers. She had even considered the possibility that the boys might have caused him to fall on the shears.

But supposing it wasn't the village youths who had been mutilating the hydrangeas? What if it was someone else, someone intent on something a good deal more serious than simple mischief? She would have to pay a visit to the library, she decided, as soon as possible. Maybe she would find her answer there.

"Cecily, perhaps we should talk of more pleasant things and divert your mind from all the troubles you have been dealt this week."

Coming back to the present with an effort, Cecily felt a pang of remorse when she saw the deep concern on Baxter's face. "I think you're absolutely right, Baxter. Do you have a subject in mind?"

"I do, as a matter of fact." He took the cup and saucer she handed him and set it by his plate.

She reached for a small silver jug and handed that to him as well, then waited while he poured the cream over his porridge. He was smiling when he handed it back to her.

She would never cease to be fascinated by his smile, she thought, as she poured cream into her bowl. She had seen barely a glimpse of it for so very long. In fact, there had been times when she wondered if he had an impairment and was unable to smile properly.

Carefully she sprinkled demerara sugar on her porridge, then stirred it gently with her spoon. "We had better eat this before it cools," she said, raising the spoon to her lips.

"I agree. And while we are eating, you can decide upon which day you wish to take our godchildren on an outing."

She hoped he hadn't noticed the slight tremble of her hand. "I'll give it some thought," she said, then popped a spoonful of porridge into her mouth.

The mixture was hot and creamy, with a faint hint of cinnamon. She had always disliked porridge until she'd tasted Michel's mastery with it. Now she looked forward to it every morning.

They ate in amiable silence for a while, then Baxter laid down his spoon. "That was excellent, as always. I really don't know if the Pennyfoot would do so well without Michel's magnificent culinary expertise. He is an integral part of this establishment."

The mention of Michel dampened Cecily's spirits. There was still that problem to deal with at some time. Sooner or later she would have to discuss it with Baxter. He had a right to know the truth about Michel's past. Together they would have to decide whether or not pursue the matter further.

Determined not to dwell on it for now, however, she said brightly, "How does next Wednesday sound to you?"

He looked at her with such intensity she felt quite unsettled. "My dear madam, any day spent with you would be a joy. I just hope I am up to the task of managing two active babies.''

She managed a light laugh. ''I can assure you, it's easier than it looks. Though I must admit to being a little out of practice myself.''

He leaned closer. ''Are you certain you want to risk such a venture with me?''

She smiled happily at him. ''I am looking forward to it with great pleasure. I can't wait to see how you handle the feedings.''

Baxter looked nervous. ''I hadn't really considered that.''

Cecily laughed at his expression. ''Don't worry, Baxter, I'll let you have Lillian—she's less rambunctious than James. Just watch what I do and copy me. All you really have to worry about is that you don't drop her.''

''Drop her?'' His eyebrows shot up. ''Perish the thought, madam. I shall endeavor to hold on to her no matter what happens. I must say, this is all sounding more difficult than I had envisioned.''

''I hate to concern you further, Baxter, but this is only the beginning. Just think how it will be as the twins grow older. Babies are a great deal easier to take care of than a three year old. A boy can be quite a handful around the age of eight or nine, and a girl can cause a great deal of worry once she reaches twelve or so.''

''Good Lord,'' Baxter muttered, looking aghast. ''I hadn't realized there was so much involved. I'm beginning to think I might have taken on more than I can handle.''

''Don't worry, Bax. You'll make a wonderful godfather. Besides, by the time the twins are at an awkward age, Gertie could very well be married and settled in a home of her own. Then she won't need us quite so much.''

Baxter rolled his eyes to the ceiling as if he sincerely doubted such an event, but refrained from commenting further.

Throughout the rest of the meal he seemed anxious to

discuss several new ideas he had for the Pennyfoot. Cecily was intrigued with his ingenuity. For someone who had opposed change for so long, Baxter had certainly come a long way.

"You once mentioned that you would like to install a telephone in the hotel," he said as they were enjoying an excellent gooseberry tart for dessert. "I think we should be able to afford it now. It will pay for itself with the time saved by having to send a messenger."

She looked at him in delight. "A telephone? How wonderful. We shall be able to take bookings with it, instead of the tiresome business of waiting for the mail to arrive and worrying if our replies will reach our guests in time."

"Precisely. After using a telephone extensively at the bank, I realize now how very useful one can be for a business."

Personally, Cecily had always thought so, but she curbed the impulse to say so.

"This has been a very pleasant meal," Baxter remarked as he laid down his serviette next to his plate.

"It has, indeed." She had truly enjoyed discussing the renovations to the hotel with him. It reminded her of when she and James had first bought the hotel. Their heads were so full of plans, most of which never came to fruition.

Now that she had a full-time partner, and one who seemed to have come to terms with the fast-changing world they lived in, perhaps some of those plans would finally be fulfilled. It was an exciting thought.

Leaving Baxter to return to his office, Cecily headed for the library. It took her several minutes to locate the book she was looking for. It stood on one of the higher shelves, and she had to drag a chair over to the wall in order to reach up for it.

After carrying the heavy tome over to the table, she sat down and opened it up. She turned immediately to the end of the book and ran a finger down the index until she found a reference to hydrangeas. Quickly she flipped the pages over until she reached the right one.

The drawing depicted a bush much like the ones that bordered the tennis courts. The huge clusters of delicate blossoms looked like rounded Chinese lanterns clinging to the boughs.

Cecily skimmed through the text, paying scant attention to the description of pale blue, lavender, and rose petals, depending on the acidity of the soil. John's hydrangeas had always been pink, no doubt due to the sandy soil.

It was the last line that captured her attention, however, and she read it twice, just to be certain.

This is one of the most poisonous of the common plants. All parts of the hydrangea, especially the flower buds, are exceptionally toxic. The poison is cyanogenetic. Symptoms of severe gastrointestinal distress occur several hours after ingestion. The effect is nearly always fatal.

Slowly Cecily closed the book. She could remember distinctly John's words. *Little blighters have been hacking off the blossoms.* They had both assumed that the damage was the result of mischief-making by the village youths. But what if someone else had wanted the blossoms? Someone who planned to poison Lord Sittingdon?

John had vowed to keep watch over his bushes. He could have unwittingly seen that person returning for more blossoms. In which case, he could well have been silenced. It would be a simple matter to place the shears in his hand to make his death appear to be an accident. John's failing strength would have made him an easy target.

Cecily rose and carried the book back to the shelves. It all seemed to fit into place. She never had truly believed that the gardener had fallen on the shears. John might have been getting on in years, but he was not careless. It seemed far more likely that John had seen a killer at work and had been silenced.

Climbing down from the chair, Cecily faced the inevitable conclusion. If the person who had poisoned Lord Sittingdon had, indeed, returned for more blossoms, that could mean only one thing. Whoever it was intended to kill again.

The questions was, who was the next intended victim? Two people had been killed already, presumably by the same hand. Obviously the murderer would not hesitate to kill again. It was up to her to discover the identity of the killer, Cecily urged herself, and as soon as possible. Or the staff of the Pennyfoot could very well have a third murder with which to contend.

She wasted no time in sending word to Samuel that she wished to go into town. Dr. Prestwick's office lay on the other side of Badgers End, and the distance was too far to walk, especially since time was of the essence.

Cecily rushed to make herself ready for the outing and hurried down the stairs a short while later, praying that Baxter would not be hovering in the lobby.

Apparently he was still poring over his accounting books, as she saw no sign of him as she crossed the floor to the front door.

Ned opened the door for her with a sweeping bow. "Going out for a breather, are we, mum? Couldn't pick a better afternoon to stroll along the Esplanade, I might say."

He flicked the brim of his braided cap with his fingers. "Wouldn't mind tripping along there meself. I do like to watch the bathing beauties frolicking in the ocean. Sight for sore eyes, as they say."

"Yes, I'm sure," Cecily murmured. "I'm expecting Samuel to fetch me in the trap, however. Would you please take a look and see if he's here yet."

"My pleasure, mum. Hang on a sec, I'll take a quick butchers." Seeing Cecily's puzzled frown, he added, "Butcher's hook, mum. Look."

He disappeared out of the door, while Cecily sent a wary

glance down the hallway. She half expected Baxter to come striding toward her, demanding to know where she was going and why she hadn't mentioned her errand to him.

Ned popped his head in the doorway and gave her a cheeky grin. "He's here, Mrs. S. Can I give you a hand down the steps, then?"

"Thank you, Ned, but I can manage quite well by myself." She swept past him, lifting the hem of her skirt to step over the threshold. She'd tied a pink chiffon scarf over her hat, since the breeze from the North Sea was quite brisk. She intended to travel with the canopy pushed back. This might be one of the last opportunities she would have to drive along the Esplanade in the sunshine this year and enjoy the sights.

Samuel assisted her into the trap, then climbed up onto his seat. "Where to, mum?" he called out.

"Dr. Prestwick's, Samuel. I shan't be long, so you can wait to bring me back."

"Yes, mum." Samuel made a clicking noise with his tongue, and the chestnut moved forward, ears pricked as the dull roar of a motorcar echoed down from the hill.

Her somber mood vanished as she looked out across the warm sands. The familiar sight of children in their straw hats, building sandcastles, bowling hoops, and flying kites, and the sound of their laughter as they huddled together in front of the tiny red-and-white-striped tent of the Punch and Judy show were infinitely comforting.

Were she ever to leave Badgers End, how she would miss the seagulls' cries as they glided across the calm waters of the bay. She never failed to count her blessings every time she felt the salty wind in her face while the chestnut's hooves clopped unevenly down the street.

She heard the motorcar draw closer, then watched it overtake the trap, making the mare toss her head in disgust as smoke belched from the exhaust with an explosive bang.

Cecily watched the blue roadster race toward the High Street with mixed feelings. While she embraced the modern changes that were taking place in the world with such breathtaking speed, she was well aware that there were prices to be paid for the new conveniences.

London was overrun with motorcars, according to the newspapers. One day that very same thing could happen here in Badgers End. They would all have to become accustomed to the smell and the noise.

In fact, they would have to become accustomed to a great many changes, she told herself as she glanced up at the sweep of Putney Downs rising beyond the sheer white cliffs. Yet some things would surely stay the same. Such as standing on the Downs and watching the Maypole dancers.

There would always be bluebells to pick in the woods, with one ear trained for the distant sound of gypsy music. People would still ice skate on Deep Willow Pond or picnic on the slopes of Lord Withergill's estate.

The summer fetes would continue to be held in the vicarage gardens, and dear Phoebe's dance troupe would perform yet another fiasco.

Most importantly of all, she thought with a quickening of her heart, Baxter had returned to her. She would share all those things with him now, rejoicing in their new relationship, filled with the hope that one day he would see fit to cement their new intimacy with a proposal of marriage.

Until then, she would make the most of this time with him. For something told her that in the years ahead, upon looking back, she would consider these precious days of uncertainty and delicious anticipation as the very best of her life.

Indeed, if it wasn't for this worrying business with Lord Sittingdon's death and the uncertainty surrounding John Thimble's demise, she would count herself among the happiest women alive.

CHAPTER

❦ 14 ❦

"Mrs. Sinclair has left the hotel?" Phoebe looked up at Ned in dismay. "Oh, dear, I really needed to talk to her. My whistler has toothache, and his jaw is quite swollen. I doubt very much if he'll be able to perform at the ball."

"Oo, that does sound a bit naughty," Ned agreed. "Nothing more miserable than a pain in your Hampsteads, that's what I say."

Phoebe, who had been talking more or less to herself, eyed Ned with distaste. "I beg your pardon?"

"Hamsteads, love. Hampstead Heath . . . teeth."

"Good Lord, man, is that any way to talk to a lady, what? What?"

The bellow had come from within the lobby. Phoebe, who was perched on the doorstep, had trouble perceiving the shadowy figure behind Ned. There was no mistaking that voice, however.

"It's quite all right, Colonel," Phoebe said, giving Ned a disdainful look as she tripped past him. "I pay scant attention to such nonsensical drivel."

"And so you should, madam. And so you should, by Jove."

Now that she could see him plainly, the colonel seemed to be having trouble with his balance. His eyelids flapped up and down at an alarming rate, a condition bestowed upon him from the effects of gunfire at close quarters.

Some of the colonel's most colorful tales were of his days in the tropics while ostensibly serving his country. It was Phoebe's considered opinion that Colonel Fortescue had spent more time serving himself from a bottle of gin than actually participating in combat.

Looking at him now, it was quite plain to see that he had imbibed more than one or two glasses of the stuff . . . which was quite disgusting considering the fact that it was at least two hours before lunch.

The colonel tipped forward onto his toes. "Good to see you, old bean. You're looking ravishing, as always. Never could resist a well titivated woman, especially one with such impeccable taste in attire as yourself."

Phoebe closed her parasol with a snap. It was gratifying to know that the man had some saving graces. "Thank you, Colonel. One must try to keep up appearances, you know."

"You do it admirably, madam. Admirably." He rocked back on his heels, at such a sharp angle Phoebe viewed him with alarm, afraid he might topple over altogether. "I say, would you care to take a stroll in the rose garden with me? I like to take a walk before lunch. Helps to sharpen the jolly old appetite, what?"

There was nothing Phoebe could care less about than strolling with the colonel in the rose garden. Since she would have to wait for Cecily to return, however, she supposed she might as well take a breath of fresh air. She enjoyed the fragrance of roses, and she could always ignore the colonel's inane ramblings. His company would be just a mite better than walking alone.

After only a few minutes of listening to him, however, Phoebe had serious doubts about the wisdom of being alone in the colonel's company. He was most erratic, jumping from one subject to another with a confusing jumble of words.

Having reached the arbor, with its fragrant trellis of climbing roses, Phoebe decided she needed a rest. She half hoped the colonel would continue on without her, but he plonked himself down on the narrow bench beside her with a loud grunt.

"Damn nice smell, those roses," Fortescue remarked, leaning back to look up at them. "Pity that gardener fellow won't be here to take care of them now."

Phoebe's ears pricked up. "Are you talking about John Thimble?"

"That's the chappie's name, yes. Damn shame, that. Nice fellow, once you got him to open his dashed mouth."

Phoebe tried valiantly to make sense of the colonel's garbled words. "What's the matter with John?" she demanded. "He isn't ill, is he?"

Fortescue uttered a hollow laugh. "Ill, madam? No, that poor blighter won't ever be ill again. That's for sure."

Phoebe was beginning to feel worried. She really liked John, though he'd never said more than two words to her at one time. He had always been most respectful, however, doffing his cap and bowing whenever he saw her. Not like some people she didn't care to mention.

"I saw what did it, old bean," Colonel Fortescue said, leaning close enough to her to almost overwhelm her with a blast of gin-laced breath. "Damn great beast it was, burning red eyes and claws as long as sabres."

Phoebe's heart began to thump most uncomfortably. She felt warm . . . too warm, and wished desperately that there had been a breeze to cool her face. "Colonel," she said faintly, "whatever are you talking about?"

"John the gardener!" the colonel suddenly bellowed.

"Didn't anyone tell you? By Jove, that was dashed bad manners, what?"

"Tell me—" Phoebe paused, aware that her voice had risen to a squeak. She cleared her throat. She wasn't at all sure she wanted to hear the rest of this. The man was quite insane, of course. Nevertheless, she had to have the rest of it now. "Tell me what?" she said more firmly.

"Why, that the poor blighter bought it, of course. That young doorman found him lying in the bushes. Shears stuck right through his blasted throat, poor devil. Blood everywhere. Must have died instantly. I wonder—"

Phoebe never heard the rest of the sentence. The next thing she knew she was flat on her back in the grass with her skirts raised at a disgusting height above her ankles. Something damp trickled down the corner of her mouth, and her throat was on fire.

The most frightening thing of all was the monster who loomed over her, blocking out the sun. Its face seemed to be framed in a white cloud. Phoebe opened her mouth to scream. She was prevented from doing so by a stream of liquid fire poured down her throat. Quite certain she was about to die, Phoebe fought off the monster with her clenched fists.

"I say, old bean, take it easy, what?"

Phoebe choked and spluttered as her vision cleared to reveal Colonel Fortescue's worried face. His white hair appeared to be standing on end, and his beard was definitely ruffled. His eyes, although bleary, were full of concern.

"Good Lord, madam, you gave me a fright. I thought I had another dead body on my hands. Saw it all the time in the tropics. Why, I remember once—"

Phoebe let out a howl of protest and struggled into a sitting position, tugging her skirts over her ankles at the same time. The front of her French lace blouse was soaked, and her head seemed to be floating a foot off her shoulders.

"Whatever did you give me?" she demanded as the colonel's bulky figure swayed in front of her.

"Gin, madam. Best medicine in the world. Always carry a spot with me. Never know when you might need it, what?"

Phoebe touched her throat gingerly with her fingers. The burning sensation had passed, leaving a warm, satisfying feeling in her stomach.

She had, on occasion, enjoyed a spoonful of brandy in her tea, generously provided by Altheda Chubb. That, too, had settled nicely in her stomach, but couldn't compare with the pleasant, fuzzy sensation that seemed to have stolen over her entire body.

"Would you pleash be so good ash to help me up, shir," she said, with as much dignity as she could muster. Unfortunately the sentence ended on a loud hiccup. Mortified, Phoebe peered up at the colonel.

He seemed not to have noticed her slip. Instead, he strode around to the back of her, thrust his hands under her armpits and quite masterfully set her on her feet.

"Thank you." Phoebe clutched the back of the bench as the ground tilted away from her. "I sheem to be having diffi . . . doffi . . . duffi . . . trouble staying on my feet. I think I'll shit down." She gasped, slapping a hand over her mouth so hard she nearly knocked herself backward. "Oh, my, did you hear what I shaid?"

"It's the gin, old girl," the colonel said gloomily. "Does that to me, too. Dashed nuisance at times. Feels like your blasted tongue is sloshing around in your mouth."

Phoebe let out a peal of laughter. She had never realized just how funny the colonel could be. Actually he was quite good company, she decided, much to her delight. She moved the tip of her tongue experimentally over her lips. Quite a pleasant taste, this gin.

She leaned forward and poked his protruding belly with a finger. "You don't happen to have any more of that . . . medishin, do you?"

*   *   *

The springs groaned in protest as the trap halted with a jerk in front of the doctor's cottage. This time Cecily waited for Samuel to assist her, even giving him a smile as she alighted. "Thank you, Samuel. I shan't be more than half an hour."

"Yes, mum." Samuel touched his cap and opened the gate for her.

She strode briskly up the path, reaching the door just as two women hurried out. They were chattering and giggling like two young girls. Eyeing their flushed cheeks, Cecily guessed that Dr. Prestwick had been bestowing his considerable charm upon the ladies again.

It was common knowledge in Badgers End that the vast majority of the good doctor's patients were female, susceptible to flattery and searching for a way to relieve their boredom. Kevin Prestwick was the answer to their prayers.

The tiny waiting room was crowded as usual, though most of the women who waited there looked as though they hadn't been ill a day in their lives.

Not that she could pass judgement, Cecily chided herself as she took a seat in the corner of the room. She herself was there today for reasons other than her health. She managed to justify that by assuring herself that her particular situation was a matter of dire importance, which was unlikely the case as far as the rest of the doctor's patients were concerned.

She was forced to watch the hands of the clock on the wall crawl for twenty agonizing minutes before Dr. Prestwick called her name.

Entering the doctor's surgery, Cecily smiled at the doctor, expecting his usual provocative greeting. To her surprise, however, his expression remained somewhat aloof and impersonal as he inquired, "I trust you are not ill, Cecily?"

"Not at all, Kevin, thank you." She settled herself in the chair in front of his desk, and waited for him to sit down. Looking at his disapproving frown, she couldn't help adding, "I wonder how busy your waiting room would be if everyone who came to see you was genuinely ill."

He grimaced. "I can hardly turn them away, no matter how petty their complaints may be."

"I suppose not." She looked around the office, determined to ease the tension that seemed to hover between them. "I see you have two new watercolors," she said brightly. "Monet, are they not?"

"Copies, of course. With my meager earnings, I could hardly afford the real thing." He picked up a pencil and began tapping it on the table. "I'm quite sure you didn't come here to discuss my paintings, however."

"No, I did not." She looked back at him, disturbed by his set expression. "It would seem that you are out of sorts this morning, Kevin. What is it they say about doctors? That they should look to their own ills as diligently as they treat others?"

"Something like that." He gave her a grave look. "I'm sorry, Cecily, if I'm not in my usual light-hearted frame of mind. One cannot be exuberant all the time."

"Indeed, I am aware of that." Feeling somewhat rebuffed, she continued, "Actually, Kevin, I came to ask you how many hydrangea blossoms would be needed in order to fatally poison a person."

Prestwick sat and stared at her for a long, uncomfortable moment. "What the devil—! Surely you're not suggesting that Lord Sittingdon was poisoned by flower blossoms?"

Cecily clasped her hands in her lap. "The thought had crossed my mind," she admitted.

Prestwick's scowl deepened.

Before he could add yet another dry comment, she hastened to explain her theory as to why John was killed. To her dismay, the longer she talked, the more testy Prestwick appeared. He made impatient noises in the back of his throat, and could hardly contain himself from interrupting her.

When she'd finally reached the end of her statement, he

actually raised his voice when he said emphatically, "John Thimble's death was an accident, purely and simply. I cannot imagine why you would think otherwise. I can only assume that you are desperate enough to conjure up this ridiculous story in order to avoid the repercussions of fatally poisoning one of your guests with contaminated food from your kitchen."

Cecily sat in stunned silence for several seconds before she recovered enough to respond. Then she straightened her back and drew in a careful breath. "Dr. Prestwick, your accusation has yet to be proven, I do believe. In the meantime, it is clearly my duty to explore all other possibilities, before making such a rash assumption."

"You have no reason to suspect foul play, Cecily. If you insist on this course, however, you should be informing the constabulary, instead of wasting my time and yours."

"As you so adroitly pointed out, I have no proof," Cecily said, doing her best to curb her temper. "Which is why I am here. John Thimble informed me that someone had been hacking off the blossoms of the hydrangeas. It occurred to me that whoever was responsible might have been collecting hydrangea blossoms to make poison, since they are deadly. I simply wanted to know if such a thing were possible, since that could be a motive for John's death."

"Yes, it is possible. But that is nonsense." Prestwick rose, indicating his desire to put an end to the conversation. "I can assure you, Cecily, that my examination of the body revealed that the shears entered the neck horizontally. I presume that the victim's hands, still holding the opened shears, hit the ground first, tilting the blades upward as the victim fell upon them."

Cecily winced. "John Thimble," she said quietly, "was a dear and trusted friend. I'd appreciate it if you would refer to him by name. Referring to him as the victim seems a sacrilege to his memory."

Prestwick sighed. "Forgive me," he said more gently. "I was speaking in official terms."

"Are you quite certain that the wound couldn't have been inflicted by someone else?"

Prestwick gave an emphatic shake of his head. "No one can be absolutely certain, of course. But in my opinion, if the wound had been made by an assailant, the perpetrator would have had to stand directly in front of Thimble. Since your gardener was below average height, and bowed with age, had anyone attacked him in that manner, the wound would have angled up or down, depending on whether it was an uppercut or downward thrust."

Cecily began to feel queasy. "In my opinion, his death was just too much of a coincidence. I feel strongly that John was killed because he disturbed someone in the act of collecting the hydrangea blossoms. In which case that person had a great deal to hide."

The doctor moved around the desk and offered his hand to Cecily. She took it, allowing him to assist her to her feet. "I certainly hope," he said quietly, "that for your sake you are mistaken in your beliefs. In any case, this should be a matter for the constabulary."

"You gave me your word you would not report this incident just yet," Cecily reminded him.

"I was wrong to do so. It is against the law to keep information from the police. It is my duty to report the death of Lord Sittingdon and the probable cause." He let go of her hand, though he softened his voice. "You have nothing to fear, Cecily. The death will be ruled as accidental poisoning. There will be no criminal charges. The only problem you have to concern yourself with is the possibility of a civil liability suit."

She shook her head. "Lady Katherine has assured me she has no wish to be involved in such a suit. She has no intention of pressing charges."

"Well, then, I would say you have emerged from this nasty business relatively unscathed. Let well alone is my advice to you." He strode to the door and opened it for her.

She paused as she reached him, and looked him in the eye. "I might be unscathed, Kevin, but someone I cared about has lost his life. I will not rest until I have the truth. In the meantime, you must do whatever you feel compelled to do. I would not want you to run afoul of the law on my account, so I release you from your promise."

Brushing by him, she stepped out into the waiting room, forestalling any further conversation. She almost felt sorry for him, however, when she saw the frustration in his eyes.

Satisfied that he would keep his promise, if only for a short while, Cecily traveled back to the hotel pondering on the doctor's uncharacteristic behavior.

No matter how strong Kevin's judgement, she was convinced that John had been killed by the same hand that had poisoned Lord Sittingdon. Now she was left with the task of proving her suspicions, and she could expect no help from Kevin Prestwick, that much was apparent.

There were, after all, several people in the hotel who had reason to hate Lord Sittingdon. Bella DelRay, for one, who surely had reason to want the aristocrat to suffer in the same manner as she had while trying to rid herself of his unwanted child.

Then there were the suffragettes to consider. They had also suffered at the hand of the dead man. It could well be that one of them simply wanted to give him a severe bellyache, never realizing that the blossoms were actually lethal. Nevertheless, whatever the intention had been, the result was certainly consequential.

Cecily glanced up at the sun. By her calculations, it must be close to noon, she decided. She had promised to meet Baxter in the roof garden to discuss the alterations. He didn't care to be kept waiting. Particularly when he discovered the reason for her tardiness.

That was the least of her worries, however. If she didn't discover the culprit's identity soon, she thought worriedly, she would have a great deal of explaining to do to Constable Northcott.

What was more important was that time was very likely running out for the murderer's intended victim. If her theories held water, whoever poisoned Lord Sittingdon also killed John Thimble in order to escape detection. The question was, who was the next victim?

CHAPTER

❈ 15 ❈

"Gertie, take this tray up to Miss DelRay's suite this instant," Mrs. Chubb called out as Gertie scurried by her on her way to the kitchen door.

Doris, who stood in her usual spot in front of the sink, lifted her head at the sound of the singer's name. She tilted her head and watched as Gertie came to an abrupt halt with a heavy sigh.

"Do I bleeding have to?" Gertie said plaintively. "I just took one up to Lady Katherine's suite. Why didn't you give it to me to take up with that one?"

"Because we didn't get the order until after you'd left, that's why. It came in late." Mrs. Chubb picked up the tray and crossed the kitchen, the keys at her belt clinking as she thrust the heavy load into Gertie's reluctant hands. "There you are, my girl. Now take it up this minute, before that soup starts getting cold."

"Bleeding hell," Gertie muttered. "I was just going out to get a breath of fresh air and all. I don't get no bloody time to do nothing nowadays, I don't. I could blinking suffocate, and no one would flipping care."

She kicked the door open with her foot so hard it slammed back against the wall.

"Gertay!" Mrs. Chubb yelled. "If that marked the wall, it's coming out of your wages, my girl."

Doris withdrew her arms from the sink and brushed off the soap bubbles. She waited until Mrs. Chubb had vanished into the pantry, then she sped across the kitchen and flew through the door.

Gertie was halfway up to the steps to the lobby when Doris caught up with her. "I'll take the tray up for you, Miss Brown," she said, taking the heavy tray from Gertie's hands. "Then you can go and get your breath of fresh air."

Gertie looked at her in surprise. "Cor blimey, ain't you the fairy bleeding godmother today. What'd I do to deserve this, then?"

"You've helped me out now and then. I thought it was about time I did something for you." Doris started up the stairs before Gertie could change her mind.

Gertie snorted. "Well, don't get too bleeding eager, or I might find a few more things for you to do."

Doris paused at the head of the stairs and looked down at her. "Perhaps you should use the back door, Miss Brown, so Mrs. Chubb doesn't see you."

"Just mind you don't drop the bleeding tray, that's all." Gertie sounded gruff, but Doris knew by her face that she was pleased with her brief escape.

Now all she had to do, Doris told herself as she reached the top of the steps, was try to talk Bella DelRay into listening to her sing. This was her big chance to make it onto the stage, and she wasn't about to let it slip through her fingers.

Humming to herself, her head full of dreams, she headed

across the lobby. Just as she reached the stairs she heard Ned's voice calling out to her.

"Where's Gertie, then?" he asked when she went back to see what he wanted. "I've been keeping an eye out for her all morning, but I ain't seen her yet."

"She's outside in the yard," Doris said, deeming it unnecessary to tell Ned that Gertie was taking a well-earned respite.

Ned sighed. "All right, per'aps you'd better give her this, then." He handed Doris a small white envelope. "It arrived this morning, but I haven't had time to get down to the kitchen to give it her."

Doris glanced at Gertie's name scrawled boldly across the envelope. Balancing the tray on the hallstand, she shoved the letter into the pocket of her apron. "I'll give it to her as soon as I get back to the kitchen," she promised.

"Ta, luv." Ned shook his head as the front door swung open. "This lot have been going in and out like bloody bees all day," he muttered, then hurried over to the door to greet the newcomers.

Doris took hold of the tray again and headed for the stairs once more. She could feel her heart thumping away, and her hands shook as she bore the food upstairs. She was on her way to see Bella DelRay again.

Maybe this would be the day the singer would hear her voice, Doris thought, feeling chills at the thought. She'd already rehearsed the song she would sing. It wasn't exactly Variety, since she hadn't heard too many of those. But it was Music Hall, and according to the woman she'd learned it from, it was quite popular in its day.

Nervously humming the melody under her breath, she concentrated on the words in her mind. She reached the top of the stairs, still preoccupied with her proposed rendition, and nearly jumped out of her skin when she saw a shadow move along the hallway.

She recognized the woman at once and jerkily bent her knees. "Good morning, Lady Katherine."

The widow moved toward her, one jeweled hand pressed to her forehead. "Thank heavens, child. I was hoping someone would come to help me. I am in such a state I can't even see straight."

Doris looked at the widow anxiously. She felt terribly sorry for the poor woman, having just lost her husband and all, though to hear some people talk, he wasn't that much of a loss. Still, it had to be so awful to watch your own husband die like that.

Lady Katherine uttered a low sob and moved closer.

Doris edged backward, hoping that the grieving woman wouldn't weep all over her shoulder and make her blouse all damp. After all, what could she possibly say to a toff that would be any help?

In spite of her chalk-white face and puffy eyes, however, Lady Katherine appeared to compose herself. "I was on my way back from the powder room," she said, "when I realized my precious pendant was missing." She grasped the lace collar at her throat with her elegant fingers. "I'm afraid the clasp must be loose. I wonder if you could help me find it? My sight is quite poor, I'm afraid, and in this dark corridor . . ."

Doris hesitated for the space of a few seconds. If she helped Lady Katherine, the soup would get cold. If she delivered the tray first and then helped look for the pendant, she might not get another chance to sing for Bella DelRay.

Deciding it was worth a complaint of cold soup, Doris looked around for somewhere to put the tray.

"You can set the tray down here," Lady Katherine said, lifting a vase of flowers from the small pedestal table. "Thank you, milady." Doris set the tray down on the table, then started looking around on the floor.

"I really am anxious about finding the pendant," Lady Katherine said from behind her. "It was my last gift from my dear late husband. An anniversary gift, and I—"

She caught back a sob, and Doris said hastily, "I'll look really hard, milady."

"I'm sure it's right here on the floor. Most likely farther down, toward the powder room."

Doris obediently began walking along the hallway, peering intently into the shadows where the light from the windows couldn't reach. In a matter of moments she spied the little heap of gold chain and sparkling diamonds lying in the corner, right next to the door of the powder room.

"Here it is," she called out and rushed back with it to the widow.

Lady Katherine pressed a handkerchief to her mouth to smother another sob. "How can I ever thank you, dear girl?" She took the pendant in her hands and held it lovingly against her cheek.

"There's no need, milady," Doris said dutifully. She lifted the tray and started to leave.

"No, no, I insist." Lady Katherine's hand hovered over the tray. "Please, take this for your trouble. You have been most helpful." Something clinked against the plate, and the widow then hurried away down the corridor to her room.

Doris looked down at the trinket lying next to Bella DelRay's lobster salad. It gleamed with a soft pink glow in the light from the sunlit windows. Doris gasped as she stared at the most beautiful pearl hatpin she'd ever set eyes upon.

She'd never had such a gift in her entire life. She set the tray back onto the table, then picked up the beautiful bauble with trembling fingers and dropped it into the pocket of her apron.

Perhaps the pin would be a lucky talisman for her, she thought with rising excitement. Maybe Bella DelRay would listen to her sing after all. She hurried down the hallway to the singer's room, more anxious than ever now to show the singer what she could do.

Wedging one edge of the tray into her hip, she raised her hand and tapped on the door. Seconds crawled by while she waited, the silverware jiggling together as the tray shook in her trembling hands.

Just when she thought she'd have to knock again, the door opened, and there stood Bella DelRay looking down at her.

"Well, goodness me, whatever's this?" she exclaimed, staring at the tray as if she'd never seen one before.

Doris felt a chill as she looked at the singer's drawn face. She really did look terribly ill. The navy blue kimono she wore was decorated with huge pink blossoms that stressed the pallor of her skin.

"It's lobster salad and mulligatawny soup, Miss DelRay," she said nervously. "I offered to bring it up to you. I'm sorry it's late. I was stopped twice on the way up here."

"But I didn't . . . I don't remember . . ." Bella's frown smoothed out. "That was terribly thoughtful of you, dearie. Thank you." She took the tray and started to close the door with her shoulder.

Doris made a small, desperate sound in the back of her throat.

Bella paused, raising her thin eyebrows. "There was something else?"

Doris cleared her throat. "Miss DelRay, I don't like to bother you, but I was wondering—" She paused, uncertain of how best to phrase her request.

"Yes? You were wondering?" Bella half-closed her eyes and swayed, as if she were about to faint.

Doris looked at her in alarm. "I was wondering if you felt well enough to listen to me sing," she said, speaking so fast her words slurred together.

The singer looked down at the tray in her hands. "I'm sorry, I really don't think—"

Trying desperately to hide her disappointment, Doris bobbed a curtsey and started to back away. "I'm sorry, Miss DelRay. I didn't mean to be a nuisance. Really I didn't. I'll go now. Please excuse me . . ."

"No, wait." Bella gave her a weary smile. "I used to be just as eager and intense as you at one time. I remember how it feels. Perhaps one song, if it won't take too long.''

Doris caught her breath. ''Oh, no, Miss DelRay, I promise I won't take up too much of your time.''

''Very well, then. Come in, and please close the door behind you.''

Doris could feel collywobbles in her stomach as she closed the door. The sitting room smelled of lavender, and she eagerly took stock of the surroundings. It was the first time she'd been inside any singer's abode, let alone someone as famous as Bella DelRay. She wanted to imprint every detail on her mind, in order to savor the memory later, when she was alone.

Her gaze fell upon a white silk dressing gown trimmed with pure white ostrich feathers, thrown carelessly across the back of the chaise lounge in the center of the room. She could just picture herself in that, as well as in the soft pink satin slippers that lay nearby.

A magazine lay open on the small table, but she couldn't quite see what it was. More than likely an entertainment magazine, she thought, making a mental note to ask one of the maids to retrieve it for her, should Miss DelRay happen to discard it.

Bella put the tray down on top of the bureau, then made her way slowly to the bed. Sinking down on the edge of it, she uttered a small sigh. ''Well, dearie, what are you going to sing for me?''

Doris could feel her mouth going dry. She licked her lips, praying she'd be able to find her voice. ''It's called, 'Don't Tell Nellie,' '' she said, looking anxiously at the singer for approval.

Bella frowned. ''Not sure I know that one. But go on. Just pretend I'm not here.''

Doris took a deep breath and opened her mouth.

The song was about a flower seller on the streets of London, who was in love with a gentleman who bought a flower from her each day to wear in his lapel. Then one day he didn't come, and Nellie waited every day after that, praying that this would be the day he'd be there. The other street sellers knew that he'd died, but no one wanted to tell Nellie that her love had passed away.

It was a sad song, and Doris gave it everything she'd got. She flung out her arms, she beat her breast, she tore at her hair and finally, when she got to the last part where Nellie finds out her love is dead and throws herself into the Thames, Doris sank in a sobbing heap onto the floor.

She stayed there, waiting in terrified silence for Bella's reaction. Finally it came.

"Well, well," Bella said softly. "That was quite a performance. Your friends were right, ducky, you can sing. I might be able to do something for you, after all."

Doris closed her eyes and began to cry quietly in earnest.

"Here, here," Bella said kindly, "don't take on so. I can't promise anything will come of it, you know. All I can do is set you up with an audition with one or two London producers. The rest will be up to you."

Doris lifted her face, tears streaming down her cheeks. "Oh, Miss DelRay, I don't know how to thank you." She scrambled to her feet, feeling as if they would never touch the floor again.

"I don't know that I'm doing you any great favors, dearie," Bella said, passing a hand wearily across her forehead. "I can only hope that you're a good deal stronger than you look. You'll need all the stamina you can muster if you want to make a name for yourself out there."

"I'll work until I drop," Doris said tearfully, clasping her hands together to keep them from shaking. "Honest I will. I'm ever so grateful, Miss DelRay—"

"Oh, call me Bella." The singer rose unsteadily, supporting herself with one hand on the edge of the bed. "It's a wicked, wicked world out there, duckie, though I've got an idea you'll be able to take care of yourself. But, just in case, keep it in mind that I'll be around if you ever need someone to talk to, all right?"

Tears started spurting from Doris's eyes again, and she

dashed them away with the back of her hand. "Thank you, Miss . . . Bella. I'll never forget what you did for me. I'll make you proud of me, you'll see. And when I'm as famous as you I'll tell everyone how good you were to me, I swear I will."

Bella laughed. "If I live that long," she said dryly. "Now go on with you, I need my rest."

"I hope the soup isn't cold," Doris said, glancing guiltily at the tray as she crossed the floor.

Bella opened the door. "Never mind about that. It wouldn't be the first time I'd eaten cold soup. I'll get a message to you when I get something set up, but don't get too worried if you don't hear from me for a while. These things take time, you know."

Doris nodded. "I'll be patient," she promised breathlessly. "I'll spend the time practicing everything I know, and I'll try and learn some new songs."

As Bella closed the door, Doris waited for a heartbeat, then leapt into the air, with a hushed shout of joy. She'd done it. She'd taken the first important step toward her dream. She'd actually got a chance to audition in London, in front of a real producer. Just wait until she told everyone.

With her heart feeling as if it would burst, she floated all the way down the stairs, rehearsing how she would tell them all that she was going to be a star like Bella DelRay.

CHAPTER

🌻 16 🌻

Cecily gasped for breath as she reached the top of the stairs that led to the roof garden. She took an extra moment or two to untie the scarf and straighten her hat, then, with a little lift of expectation, she pushed open the door.

Sunlight flooded the steps and momentarily blinded her. She closed her eyes briefly, then stepped out into the cool, fragrant breeze from the ocean.

Baxter stood with his back to her, staring out over the wall toward the sea with a stillness about him that disturbed her. Worried that he might be angry with her, she said tentatively, "Baxter?"

He swung around at once and, to her immense relief, gave her one of his rare smiles. "There you are. I was beginning to worry about you."

"I'm so sorry I'm late." She walked toward him, her

heart lifting as it always did when she saw him. "I had an errand to run."

"No need to apologize. I rather enjoyed the solitude."

She lifted an eyebrow. "Would you prefer I leave you alone?"

He reached for her hand and drew her closer. "Not at all, as you well know. And as long as we are alone . . ." He bent his head and kissed her, managing to render her speechless for a moment or two.

When she had recovered sufficiently to speak, she said lightly, "You appeared to be deep in thought when I arrived. I trust you are not having second thoughts now?"

"Not about our partnership, I can assure you. In fact, I was wondering if you were planning to make a formal announcement."

Taken aback, she stared up at him. "Do you think we should?"

"You have always treated your staff as a family. Don't you want them to know that our status has changed?"

Aware that this was a sensitive issue, Cecily said quickly, "I have informed Phoebe and Madeline, of course. I just hadn't thought about an announcement, with everything else on my mind. I'm sorry, Bax. Of course you're right. I shall gather the staff together tomorrow morning. I hope you will stand with me as I make the formal announcement."

"I shall be happy to, dear madam."

That settled, Cecily looked around the tiny garden. "What do you think we should do with the rose barrels?"

He looked pensive as he gazed at her. "Are you quite certain you want to change things up here? After all, now that John has gone . . ." He left the sentence dangling, and she moved over to the wall.

From where she stood she could see the sweep of the bay, with the fishing boats anchored in the harbor and the tiny thatched cottages that lined the rocky coast. Several late-summer visitors strolled along the sands and down the

Esplanade, where the wind stirred up the leaves from the sycamore trees that lined the promenade.

Already she could feel the promise of winter's chill in the air. Soon the visitors would be gone, and the Esplanade would be deserted. She had always looked forward to this time, to the quiet months when the weekend guests took over and gave everyone time to breathe during the peaceful, dark, winter weekdays.

James had loved the off season, and the opportunity for them to spend more time together. But now James was gone, and it was time to erase the past.

"I'm quite sure," she said firmly.

She started when she felt Baxter's hands on her shoulders. "I understand how you feel, Cecily. I'll quite understand if you want to leave things the way they are."

She turned sharply to face him. "No, Bax. I want this to be our garden, without the ghost of James anywhere in it. I want to get rid of the barrels and use boxed planters instead. I don't want roses up here. The roof garden always smelled of roses. Just as soon as we hire a new gardener, this will be his first assignment." And her last farewell to James, she added inwardly. This time she felt no qualms about it. It was time.

"I'm getting butterflies in my stomach," Ethel complained as she set out the silver sugar bowls on the kitchen table.

"More'n likely that bleeding Scotch egg you ate for lunch," Gertie said, wiping away a tear. She held the half-peeled onion away from her face and sniffed loudly.

"It's not that," Ethel said scathingly. "It's fright, that's what it is."

Gertie looked at her from watery eyes. "What are you bloody frightened about?"

"What we're going to do tonight, that's what." Ethel shot a look over at the door. "I keep wondering what they'll do to us when they see us. What if they attack us?"

Gertie sniffed again and wiped her nose on her sleeve.

"I'd like to see them try. Don't be bleeding daft, Ethel. They won't attack us. I already bloody told you that over and over again."

"I know." Ethel picked up a fat, white, enameled bin and began pouring the brown sugar carefully into the little bowls. "I just wish that Miss Atkins and Miss Croft were coming with us. They'd know what to do if something bad happened."

"Yeah," Gertie said, talking through her stuffed-up nose. "Bleeding run like hell, with the bloody rest of us."

Ethel looked up. "You don't really think there'll be trouble, do you? My Joe would go berserk if something bad happened to me, I know he would. He'd never forgive me."

Gertie sighed. "Will you bleeding stop whining about what's going to happen? Nothing bleeding bad is going to happen, all right? That Sid Flemming what owns the pub is a nice chap, and he won't let nothing bad happen to us, I know."

"How'd you know he's nice?" Ethel demanded. "I didn't know you'd met him."

"I haven't, have I. But Ned has, and he told me all about him. Ned says as how we'll be all right as long as Sid was there." She attacked the onion again. "Besides," she mumbled, "Ned's going to bloody be there, too, just to make sure nothing does happen, so you ain't got nothing to worry about, have you."

Ethel slapped the sack down on the table. "Gertie Brown, you promised you wouldn't tell no one what we planned to do."

Gertie shrugged. "Ah, Ned's all right, ain't he. You bleeding worry too much, Ethel. You never used to be like this before you got bleeding well married. That Joe's took all your flipping guts away, that he has."

Ethel bit back a retort and went on filling the sugar bowls. The truth was, the closer it got to the evening, the more sure she was that she didn't want to go down the George and Dragon. She wanted to go home, where it was all nice and safe, with Joe. Somehow, now that she had him, adventures weren't what they used to be.

Carefully she sliced a vanilla bean in half and pushed the two pieces into the sugar. She couldn't back down now, though, she told herself. It was all set up, and she couldn't let the rest of them down. As Gertie had said, they needed all the help they could get to carry out their plan, and there would be only four of them as it was.

She'd just have to explain to Joe if he found out. She'd tell him that she felt obligated to go with the rest of them, and that she hadn't told him about the plan before because she didn't want him to worry about her. She hoped that would be enough to calm him down.

Joe Salter was the kindest, most understanding, most generous man she'd ever met, but he had a wicked temper when he was crossed.

She shuddered, wondering if she was more scared of what the men at the George and Dragon might do or of Joe, and what he'd do to her if he found out where she'd been.

The door opened, and thinking it was Doris coming back with the empty trays, Ethel didn't bother to look up. Apparently Gertie was too busy wiping her eyes to see who it was, because when Madam spoke, she muttered a quiet "Bleeding heck," before adding more loudly, "Good afternoon, mum. What can we do for you?"

Ethel, startled by Madam's rare appearance in the kitchen, dropped the sack of sugar. Some of its contents spilled across the table in a heap of sparkling brown crumbs.

"Ah, there you are, Gertie," Cecily said as she walked farther into the kitchen. "I wanted to have a word with you if you have a minute?"

Gertie dropped the onion in the sink, then lifted the skirt of her apron to wipe away the tears. "Yes, mum, 'course I got a minute."

"I was just wondering," Cecily said, "if you remember

when you met Miss Atkins and Miss Croft on the stairs the
other night. Did you happen to notice if they were carrying
flowers?''

Gertie's eyes widened. ''Flowers? No, mum, I don't remember seeing any. Like I told you, they was both talking
ten to the dozen, so I didn't really take much notice of what
they was carrying. But I'm sure I would have noticed flowers.''

Cecily nodded. ''Well, I just wondered, that's all.'' She
turned to go, just as Doris came bursting through the door.
The maid pulled up short, narrowly avoiding a nasty col-
lision.

''Please excuse me, mum,'' Doris said, dropping a deep
curtsey. Her cheeks were flushed, and her eyes sparkled
with unmistakable excitement.

Cecily regarded her curiously, wondering if perhaps
Doris had enjoyed a romantic encounter with someone. She
was still glowing herself from her own romantic encounter
with Baxter earlier.

''Something interesting must have happened to put that
radiant glow on your face, Doris,'' she said, wondering if
Samuel might have been the cause.

''Oh, it did, mum,'' Doris said happily. ''I sang for Miss
Bella DelRay this afternoon, and she said as how she could
get me an audition with a producer in London.'' She flung
out her arms and wrapped them around her body. ''Oh,
mum, I'm really going to be a singing star!''

Cecily felt a pang of apprehension. She hoped that Bella
DelRay hadn't been filling the child's head with a host of
empty dreams. ''I'm very happy for you, Doris,'' she said
cautiously. ''I hope your plans materialize for you as well
as you expect.''

''Oh, they will, mum,'' Doris said earnestly. ''I mean to
make them happen. It was awfully nice of Miss DelRay to
get me auditions, but like she said, I have to do the rest.''

"Well, I'm sure Miss DelRay knows what she is talking about."

Cecily made a move toward the door, but then Doris said quietly, "I do hope she's not ill, that's all. I'm worried about her."

Cecily paused, her hand on the door. "What do you mean?"

"Well, I took a tray up for her a while ago, but when I went up just now to fetch it, she didn't answer my knock."

"Miss DelRay most likely went out for a walk," Cecily said, opening the door.

"She didn't look like she could walk across the room when I saw her a while ago," Doris said, looking anxious. "She looked really ill and kept saying how awfully tired she was. She didn't even remember that she'd ordered the tray I took up."

Cecily froze. "She didn't remember?"

Doris shook her head. "No, she acted as if she'd never ordered it."

"That's strange," Gertie said from across the room. "How could she bloody forget when she ordered it right before you took it up to her?"

"I don't know, Miss Brown," Doris said with a shrug. "Like I said, she must be ill."

Ill, Cecily silently echoed with rising apprehension. *Dear God, not Bella DelRay.*

"Tell me, Doris," she said urgently, "did you happen to meet anyone on the way to Miss DelRay's room?"

Doris looked a little scared. "Well, mum, Ned stopped me on the way up." She slapped a hand over her mouth to smother a gasp. "Oh, cripes, I forgot all about it."

"Forgot about what?" Cecily demanded.

"Nothing, mum." Doris shot a nervous glance at Gertie. "It were just something Ned said, that's all. It weren't important."

"Did anyone else speak to you?"

"Yes, mum. Lady Katherine."

Cecily listened while Doris described how she'd searched for the pendant. "Lady Katherine was really pleased when I found it," the housemaid said, sending another look at Gertie. "Then I took the tray to Miss DelRay." She looked anxiously up at Cecily. "I explained why the soup was cold, mum, and she didn't seem to mind at all."

"Where is Mrs. Chubb?" Cecily asked, her tone sharp with anxiety.

Doris jumped. "I dunno, mum."

"She's in her room, mum," Gertie piped up. "She's taking a nap 'cos she's watching the babies for me tonight."

"Then I'm afraid I'll have to disturb her." Cecily left the kitchen and headed down the narrow passageway to the housekeeper's tiny sitting room tucked under the stairs.

She tapped on the door, waited until she heard a sleepy voice call out, "Who is it?" then opened the door.

Mrs. Chubb was just rising from her chair. A ball of pink wool rolled off her lap from the length of knitting she held, and Cecily bent to retrieve it.

"Oh, goodness, mum, thank you," Mrs. Chubb said, sounding flustered. "I didn't realize it was you. If I had I would never—"

"Don't worry, Altheda." Cecily stepped inside the tiny room. "I've come to ask you about the tray that was sent up to Bella DelRay's room. Can you tell me who ordered it?"

"Well, it's funny you should mention that, mum. I thought it was a bit strange myself. It wasn't with the usual orders. One of the footmen must have brought it in and left it on the spike in the kitchen, though it's funny nobody saw him."

"Mrs. Chubb, I'd like to borrow your keys if I may?" Cecily held out her hand, and the housekeeper unfastened the ring of keys from her belt.

"There isn't any trouble, I hope, mum?" she said as she handed them to Cecily.

"Let us hope not. I'll return these to you as soon as possible." Without waiting for an answer, Cecily made for the stairs. She hoped with all her heart that Bella had simply decided to go out for a stroll.

She didn't want to consider the possibility that the singer could well be lying on her bed, dying from the same poison that had killed Lord Sittingdon.

With her heartbeat quickening at each step, Cecily climbed the second flight of stairs to the top floor. The hallway was empty as she started down it, for which she was thankful. She didn't need a witness if her worst fears were realized.

Reaching the door of Miss DelRay's suite, she rapped lightly, then waited, tapping her foot in her anxiety. She allowed several seconds to pass before rapping again, much harder this time.

Hearing no response from within, Cecily threw all caution to the winds and pounded on the door with her fist. "Miss DelRay?" she called out, hoping no one else could hear her. "Are you in there? This is Mrs. Sinclair. Would you please open the door?"

Again she waited, hearing only the faint sputtering of the gas lamps on the wall. She had no choice now, she assured herself. She had to know if the singer was all right.

Carefully she fitted the key into the lock and turned it. Holding her breath, she eased the door open and peered inside. Then her breath came out in a gasp as she caught sight of the still figure lying on the bed.

"Miss DelRay?" she said urgently. "Are you all right?"

There was no movement at all from the bed. Feeling her stomach churning now, Cecily stepped inside the room and closed the door behind her.

CHAPTER
❦ 17 ❦

Cecily moved cautiously toward the bed, watching in vain for some kind of movement from the still form. She drew close enough to look upon Bella DelRay's face and thought she saw an almost imperceptible fluttering of eyelashes. Nursing the faint hope, she reached out and touched the limp arm flung across the singer's body.

Even as Bella moved, Cecily's gaze fell upon the tray sitting on the bureau. The lobster salad, at least, looked as if it hadn't been touched.

"Mrs. Sinclair! Whatever are you doing here?" Bella sat up, pulling small wads of cotton wool from her ears as she did so.

"Please forgive me for this intrusion," Cecily said, relief making her voice tremble slightly. "Since I received no answer when I knocked, I thought you might . . . be in need of some assistance."

Bella shook her head. "I always sleep with this in my ears." She held up the cotton wool. "Can't hear a blessed thing, but it's the only way I can get proper rest in the daytime. When you work at night the way I do, you have to get used to sleeping when everyone else is awake."

"Well, I'm certainly relieved to know that you are all right." Cecily glanced over at the tray. "I see you didn't finish your lunch. I do hope there was nothing wrong with the salad?"

Bella sighed. "I couldn't touch a bite, I'm afraid. I haven't been able to eat properly since . . ." She paused, shrugging her shoulders. "Well, I daresay I'll get my appetite back eventually. Anyway, I'm sorry about the waste, although I'm quite sure I didn't order the tray. Someone must have sent it up by mistake."

"That happens now and then." Cecily picked up the tray from the bureau. "As long as I'm here, I'll take it down with me. It will save one of the maids a trip."

She had reached the door before Bella said quietly, "You didn't say why you wanted to see me, Mrs. Sinclair."

Cecily looked back at her and smiled. "I didn't, did I? I was just calling on you to make sure you were recovering from your recent . . . illness. My guests' well-being is of great concern to me."

"That's very kind of you, Mrs. Sinclair. I can assure you I am improving with every hour. In fact, I expect to be returning to London tomorrow."

"That is good news." Cecily hesitated, then decided she might as well take advantage of the moment. "I understand you have promised one of my maids that you will arrange an audition for her in London."

Bella's expression changed. "Ah, I thought there was more to it. You're worried about Doris, is that it?"

"I look upon my staff as my family, Miss DelRay. I wouldn't want the child disappointed. She has set her heart on a singing career, and I am well aware of the pitfalls of the entertainment business. She will find it difficult enough without dealing with empty promises, no matter how well-meant.''

Bella looked offended. ''That was no empty promise, Mrs. Sinclair, I do assure you. The child is a born performer and has the voice to back her up. I can't guarantee her success and I took care to tell her that. She does show a lot of promise, however, and I fully intend to approach a friend of mine who just happens to be a producer. I'm quite sure he will give her an audition. He respects my opinion.''

''As I do, Miss DelRay. I am merely looking after the interests of a member of my staff.''

Bella held her scowl for a second or two longer, then relented. ''You are to be commended, Mrs. Sinclair. Not too many employers treat their workers with such consideration. The members of your staff are very lucky.''

''They repay me, Miss DelRay, in many ways.''

''I'm sure they do.'' Bella smiled. ''Don't worry about Doris, Mrs. Sinclair. I promised to keep an eye on her and I will. She's a splendid little trouper, and I'll enjoy taking her under my wing.''

Reassured, Cecily returned the smile. ''I appreciate that, Miss DelRay. In the meantime, if there is anything we can do for you, please don't hesitate to ask.''

''Thank you, I'll do that.''

Carefully Cecily maneuvered through the door and closed it, the tray balanced on her hip. She was anxious now to get back to the kitchen. Michel should be arriving at any minute, and she wanted a word with him.

Halfway down the stairs she saw Colonel Fortescue on his way up. It was too late to turn back. All she could hope was that the colonel had drunk enough gin with lunch to render him too sleepy to socialize.

Watching the portly gentleman stagger from one side of the staircase to the other, it would seem that her wish might be granted.

''I say, old girl, what have you got there?'' Fortescue demanded as she drew closer. ''You shouldn't be doing the maid's work, by George. You've got blashted lackeys to do that, what? What?''

Cecily gave him a faint smile. ''How are you, Colonel? Enjoyed your meal, I trust?''

''Meal? Did I?'' The colonel looked confused. ''I sh'pose I did, old bean. Can't remember, to tell the truth.'' He looked at the tray. ''I'll take that lobshter up with me, though. Looks scrumpsh . . . scrumpsh . . . looks tashty.'' He reached out an unsteady hand, and Cecily whisked the tray out of reach.

''I'm sorry, Colonel, this is on its way to the kitchen. I can have a fresh one sent up to your room if you like.''

''What?'' The colonel swayed, grabbed hold of the banisters, and blinked rapidly at her with bloodshot eyes. ''Fresh one? By Jove, that's an exshellent idea. Could do with a fresh bottle of gin, yesh indeed. By the way, old girl, I shent dear old Phoebe home with Shamuel. Hope thash okay?''

Cecily stared at him. ''Phoebe? She was here?''

''Yesh, old bean. Bit under the weather, I'm afraid. Shent her home.'' He hiccuped, excused himself, then staggered past her up the stairs.

Staring after him, Cecily wondered just when he had started calling Phoebe by her Christian name. She hoped that whatever had stricken her friend, it wasn't serious. She would have to make sure to call in on her later. Sighing, Cecily continued on her way.

Reaching the kitchen at last, she nudged the door open with her hip. Mrs. Chubb was at the kitchen table, kneading a large mound of dough. She looked up, an expression of horror crossing her face when she saw Cecily.

''Madam! Whatever next! Where are those lazy girls, then? Fancy them letting you carry that—''

Cecily rested the tray on the edge of the table. ''It's perfectly all right, Altheda. I wanted to bring it down myself. Has Michel arrived yet?''

"Yes, mum, he's in the pantry sorting out the pheasants. Won't let no one touch them, he won't."

Cecily nodded. "Good. I want him to take a look at this tray."

Mrs. Chubb looked alarmed. "Nothing wrong with it, is there, mum? Where did it come from, then?"

"I've just collected it from Miss DelRay's room," Cecily said, crossing the kitchen to the pantry.

"Oh, my goodness, I set that one up myself," Mrs. Chubb wailed.

Cecily looked back at her. "Please don't upset yourself, Altheda. Whatever might be amiss with this tray is certainly none of your doing."

She found Michel in the pantry, examining the fowl that hung from hooks in the ceiling. He looked worried when she asked him to examine the food on the tray.

"I did not touch this tray, *madame,* I swear it. On my word of honor."

"I know you didn't, Michel," Cecily said soothingly. "I just want you to inspect the meal and tell me if you notice anything different about it."

His expression changed. He leaned forward and whispered hoarsely, "It is poisoned?"

"I don't know," Cecily whispered back. "I was hoping you'd be able to tell me."

Michel clutched his throat. "*Sacré bleu!*"

"There is no need to taste it," Cecily said quietly. "Perhaps you can simply smell it?"

Looking as if he would rather touch a snake, Michel lifted the cover from the soup, closed his eyes, lowered his nose and sniffed. Then, with an agonized look on his face, he dipped the tip of his little finger into the soup and touched it to his tongue.

"Well?" Cecily asked anxiously.

Michel shook his head. "I cannot taste anything different. It tastes just like my mulligatawny soup."

"What about the salad?" Cecily urged.

Michel picked up the fork that lay on the tray and poked around in the salad. Then he muttered a soft exclamation and peered closer.

"What is it?" Cecily demanded.

"Something strange," Michel murmured. "Here . . . and here." He raised the fork with pieces of the pinkish leaves clinging to the prongs. "What eez this? I do not put this in my salad. It looks like it is . . ." He pulled the leaves apart with an exclamation of disgust. "Flower petals! Who is it who plays this stupid joke?"

"It's no joke, Michel," Cecily said grimly.

He looked at her in horror. "*Mon Dieu!* You cannot mean . . . ?"

She nodded. "Please, Michel, not a word to anyone. It's imperative to keep this quiet until we have uncovered the culprit."

Michel, looking considerably shaken, passed his fingers horizontally across his lips. "Mum's the word," he said in a thick Cockney accent.

"Can you keep this salad in a safe place for now?" she asked him, feeling a little more secure when he nodded.

"Leave it with me, *madame,*" he said quietly. "No one will touch it."

"Thank you, Michel." She hurried from the pantry, smiling at a worried-looking Mrs. Chubb. "Thank you, Altheda. Please don't concern yourself about the tray. Michel is taking care of it."

"Was it poisoned?" Mrs. Chubb asked, her lips barely moving.

Cecily raised her eyebrows. "Why, Altheda," she said lightly, "whatever made you think that?"

The housekeeper sent a nervous glance at the pantry door. "I thought, perhaps, when you took that tray in—"

"I promise you, Altheda, you have nothing to worry about. Now, while I am here I want to ask for your assistance. I would like as many of the staff as possible to be present in the ballroom at eleven o'clock tomorrow morning. I have one or two announcements to make.''

Mrs. Chubb's worried frown intensified. ''I'll take care of it, mum.''

Knowing that the housekeeper would not rest until she found out what exactly was going on, Cecily flew out of the kitchen before Mrs. Chubb could question her further.

Baxter, as she expected, was in his office when she arrived there a few minutes later. With his head bent low over the ledger spread out in front of him, he looked most industrious. He looked up as she entered, after the barest of taps on the door.

Rising to his feet, he said in an injured tone, ''I was wondering when you would be here.''

Remembering that she had promised to assist him with the accounts, she hastened to apologize. ''I'm so sorry, Baxter. I'm afraid I had to take care of a rather serious matter.''

''Oh?'' He narrowed his eyes as he looked at her. ''Would this have anything to do with Lord Sittingdon?''

''Of course not,'' she said feeling ridiculously guilty. She seated herself in the leather armchair. ''While I think of it, I have set up the staff meeting for eleven o'clock tomorrow morning,'' she told him. ''I trust I can count on you to be there?''

''Of course. I wouldn't miss this meeting for the world.''

Cecily smiled. ''I wonder how many people will be truly surprised.''

''Most likely none at all, considering how swiftly news travels around this hotel.''

''Nevertheless, I should like to make it official. I understand the rumors about our relationship have been most speculative.''

''Then it's high time we put the rumors to rest.''

''I agree.''

''Good. Now will you inform me as to what kept you from assisting me with these wretched accounts?''

''I was just about to tell you.'' She leaned back, pausing

a moment to reflect on the best way to tell him what she wanted to say. "I think I might have discovered who killed Lord Sittingdon," she said at last.

Baxter dropped the pen back into the inkwell, his eyes widening as he stared at her. "Good Lord, Cecily, why didn't you tell me before?"

"Because I don't really have any proof." She sighed. "In fact, I'm afraid it might be very difficult to prove such a thing."

"Who do you think killed him, then?"

She leaned forward again, lowering her voice in spite of the fact that no one could possibly hear her. "I do believe that Lady Katherine killed her husband. I believe she poisoned him, adding the stuff to his salad after the tray was brought to the room."

Baxter looked horrified. "Why on earth would she want to do that?"

"Because she found out about his association with Bella DelRay. No doubt she discovered that Bella was bearing his child."

"But that's preposterous! I cannot believe that Lord Sittingdon would have had such an association with an . . . entertainer."

Cecily lifted her chin. "That part of it, at least, happens to be fact. Bella admitted as much to me herself."

"Miss DelRay told you she was carrying Lord Sittingdon's child?" Baxter echoed in disbelief.

"Yes," Cecily said patiently. "You see, Madeline brought a potion here to the hotel for Bella, intended to cause an abortion. She told me about it. When Bella became ill later, I told her what I knew, and she admitted it."

"Good Lord, Cecily, what are you saying? That Miss Pengrath supplied Miss DelRay with a potion to kill her child? That is unthinkable."

"To a man, no doubt," Cecily agreed. "And to some women as well, I suppose. But in Bella's case, I can understand her predicament. Lord Sittingdon had no intention of caring for her or his illegitimate child. Bella stood to lose her career and would have been left with no means of support for the child. She saw it as a kindness, in a way.''

''And you condone this?''

Cecily shook her head. ''I must admit, I would find it difficult to justify such an act. Though it's hard to say what one would do in similar circumstances.''

''But how do you think Lady Katherine came to learn about this?''

''That I don't know. I do know that she arranged the visit to the hotel. I also happen to believe that she intends to kill Bella as well.''

Baxter muttered a quiet oath. ''I find this all impossible to accept. How do you know all this?''

Cecily sighed. ''That's just the point. I don't know. I am only surmising. Lady Katherine told me herself that she arranged the visit to the hotel, supposedly for an anniversary celebration. I believe she learned that Bella intended to come down here, though it's doubtful she knew that Bella intended to rid herself of the baby.''

''But what makes you think she poisoned her husband?''

''Amongst other things, the empty plates. Michel told me all the dishes from the Sittingdon's suite were scraped clean when they arrived back in the kitchen, yet Lady Katherine told me later that she didn't eat her lobster salad because it didn't taste very good.''

''Perhaps her husband ate it.''

Cecily shook her head. ''Lady Katherine said she sent the salad back to the kitchen. I can't imagine why she would lie about that, unless she intended to cast suspicion on Michel's food.''

Baxter stood and moved over to the window, where he looked out for a long moment before speaking. ''There isn't a great deal to support your suspicions.''

''I know.'' Cecily was quiet for a moment. ''In fact, I might have given up on the entire situation, had it not been for the fact that Michel found hydrangea blossoms mixed into Bella's lobster salad.'' She paused, then added deliberately, ''Did you know that hydrangea blossoms are poisonous?''

Baxter swung around, a startled expression on his face. ''Hydrangea blossoms?'' he repeated slowly.

''Yes, Baxter,'' Cecily said firmly. ''Hydrangea blossoms. I looked it up in an old medicinal book. Hydrangeas are poisonous. And quite deadly, I might add.''

''Then . . . John Thimble?''

''Ah,'' she said with great satisfaction. ''I see you have made the connection.''

Baxter shook his head. ''This is all too much. Are you suggesting that someone deliberately killed John?''

''Not someone, Baxter,'' Cecily said softly. ''Lady Katherine.''

CHAPTER
❧ 18 ❧

"That's impossible," Baxter said abruptly. "John might have been frail, but I simply cannot imagine a woman of Lady Katherine's slight stature attacking our gardener with a pair of shears."

"I don't think she attacked him," Cecily said mildly. "I think Dr. Prestwick was quite correct when he said that John fell upon the shears. I do think that perhaps Lady Katherine pushed him from behind, hard enough to send him sprawling, so that he wouldn't recognize the person who'd been picking the blossoms from his hydrangea bushes."

"But that was after Lord Sittingdon had died," Baxter said, frowning at her.

"Precisely. Which led me to believe that whoever killed Lord Sittingdon intended to kill someone else. Then, when Doris told me that she'd met Lady Katherine on the stairs while taking a tray up to Bella, everything seemed to fall together. Especially when Doris said that she didn't think Bella had ordered the tray.''

Baxter gave her one of his penetrating looks. "You suspected there might be another murder?"

"Yes," Cecily said warily. "I did."

"And you somehow neglected to tell me about it."

Cecily shrugged. "I knew you'd be overly concerned and . . ."

"Insist that you inform the constabulary at once."

"Something like that, I suppose."

Baxter moved back to the desk and sat down. "This aptitude of yours to charge headlong into a dangerous situation, blithely ignoring the consequences, quite frankly terrifies me. I must insist that in future, if you must pursue this precarious habit, you at least enlist my help."

"I usually do at some point or other."

"Not until after you have thoroughly endangered yourself, as a rule. In future, if you are compelled to go chasing after killers and thieves, I want to know about it. I'm asking for your promise, Cecily."

"I will promise, Baxter, on one condition. That you promise me you will respect my wishes if I feel it necessary to keep certain information to ourselves in order to protect the hotel and its staff."

He studied her for a long time, then sat back in his chair. "I have a feeling that I shall live to regret this, but yes, I give you my promise."

She smiled at him, delighted at his capitulation. "Then it is settled."

"You were saying that Miss DelRay did not order the tray that was sent up to her?"

"Yes. I think Lady Katherine ordered it for her. She had ordered one for herself earlier. She most likely approached one of the footmen with an order for Bella's tray. The footman wouldn't normally read it—he'd simply put the order on the spike in the kitchen. No one would realize that Lady

Katherine had actually ordered a meal twice.''

Baxter picked up a pencil and appeared to study it for several seconds. ''How was it that Doris didn't see Lady Katherine put the blossoms in the food?''

''Doris, it appears, was too busy searching for a very conveniently lost pendant. It would be simple enough for Lady Katherine to order the tray, wait for Doris to bring it up, then distract her long enough to mix in the poison. Luckily Bella wasn't hungry and didn't eat the food.''

''What did she do with it?''

''I took it back to the kitchen and had Michel look at it.'' She couldn't help the little note of satisfaction that crept into her voice. ''He found the blossoms mixed in with the salad. I made him promise not to say anything to anyone until I'd had a chance to apprehend the culprit.''

Baxter raised his eyebrows. ''How do you propose to do that when you have no proof?''

''I don't know,'' Cecily admitted. ''I have to work on the solution to that.''

Baxter rolled his eyes up toward the ceiling. ''I knew I would regret that ridiculous promise. I don't suppose you would consider passing your theory along to the constabulary?''

She shook her head. ''If P. C. Northcott botches things up as usual and fails to prove anything, word will no doubt be spread around that the food at the Pennyfoot can, and has been, lethal. The reputation of the hotel will be destroyed, after all the hard work and effort that we have put in to make the Pennyfoot one of the most respected establishments on the coast of England. We cannot let that happen.''

Baxter frowned. ''Cecily, I would not wish anyone to defile the hotel's fine reputation, you must be assured of that. But consider this. If we attempt to resolve this matter without the proper authority, we could very well bring about the thing you fear the most.''

''I'm well aware of that.'' Cecily rose to her feet and

moved to the door. "I realize we'll have only one chance to prove my theories. If we accuse Lady Katherine without that proof, we might as well close the Pennyfoot down. That's why I have to make sure the plan is a good one."

"Whatever you decide to do, Cecily, I trust you will remember your promise and confide in me first. You must be aware that if Lady Katherine is guilty of these crimes, then she could be extremely dangerous. We will have to use the utmost caution."

She smiled fondly at him. "I assure you, I will not take any more risks on my own. If I can think of a plan that might work, I'll discuss it with you, as I promised."

He appeared to be reassured by her words, and she left him, her mind already working on a possible solution.

"Now," Gertie said, to the little group huddled about her, "you all know what we're going to bleeding do, all right?"

Doris shivered and drew her shawl closer around her shoulders. "I wish I'd worn a cardigan. It's getting cold at night now."

Gertie cast a discriminating eye at the mist coiling in from the sea. "It's that bloody time of year, ain't it? 'Course it's getting cold. It'll be flipping warm in the pub when we get down there, though."

"I'll be cold while we get there, Miss Brown," Doris complained.

Gertie looked down the Esplanade to where the street lamps in the High Street twinkled in the darkness. Between them and the hotel lay a very long, dark walk.

She would have liked to ask Samuel to take them in the trap, but if Samuel knew they were headed for the pub without an escort, he'd have not only refused to take them, but also would most likely have marched right into the Pennyfoot and told Mrs. Chubb what they planned to do.

Mrs. Chubb would put her foot down, and that would be bleeding that, Gertie thought. No, there was nothing for it but to bloody hoof it all the way.

"We'll walk quickly, that'll keep you flipping warm," Gertie told Doris briskly. "Now stop your bleeding whining. We all got to concentrate on what we're going to say."

"I thought you were going to do all the talking," Ethel said, fastening her scarf tighter over her hat.

"Not bloody likely." Gertie confronted the little group. "We're all going to take flipping turns saying what we bleeding came to say. We'll rehearse it as we go down the road. Come on."

She set off, striking out with a determined step, hoping the rest of them felt more confident than she did.

"Are we going to order drinks?" Daisy said, hugging her body with both arms as she trudged alongside the railings.

"If you like." Gertie grinned and smacked her lips in anticipation. "It's been a long time since I had a bleeding beer. I've almost forgotten what it tastes like."

Doris's mouth dropped open. "You've tasted ale? I didn't know women could drink it."

"Well, it were stout, as a matter of fact. Bloody strong it were, too." Gertie grinned at the memory. "Near on knocked me off me blinking chair, it did."

No one answered her, and the sounds of the night took over in the sudden silence. The tide had come in, and the swish of waves gently washed the darkened shore. Dry leaves rustled about their feet, and the clacking of their heels echoed across the empty sand as the moon slid behind a cloud, darkening the shadows that crept along the street with them.

"Listen," Ethel said, looking nervously over her shoulder. "What's that?"

"Don't you bleeding start," Gertie said crossly. Her nerves were jumpy enough, she thought, without Ethel's vivid imagination stirring up visions of ghosts and Gawd knows what else.

"I hear it, too, Miss Brown," Doris whispered. "It sounds like the clanking of chains."

"More like the creaking of trap springs," Daisy said in her sensible voice.

Almost immediately, the cluttering clop of hooves broke the quiet peace. "Christ," Gertie muttered. "It's that bleeding Samuel."

All four of them looked back, just as the trap emerged from the stable gate, drawn by the chestnut with Samuel leading its head.

"Now what?" Ethel demanded, coming to a complete stop.

"We tell him to mind his own bleeding business," Gertie said stoutly.

They waited in silence for Samuel to climb into the trap and draw level with them. He hauled in the reins, then peered down at them just as the moon emerged, bathing him in a ghostly light.

"If you're going to the George," he said quietly, "you'd better hop in."

Gertie stared at him in silence for a long moment. "All right, ladies," she said at last, "we might as well bleeding ride."

Samuel waited without a word as all four of them clambered aboard. It was a tight squeeze, but they finally got settled, and Samuel flicked the reins across the chestnut's back.

As the mare began plodding slowly along the Esplanade, Gertie leaned forward and demanded, "How the flipping heck did you know we was going to the George?"

"Ned told me." Samuel glanced back at them, his gaze lingering on Doris's face. "He thought if there was trouble he might need some help."

"What kind of trouble?" Ethel asked nervously.

"You really don't think you can walk into the public bar of the George and challenge the yobs to a darts game and not have trouble?" Samuel made a thick sound of disgust in his throat. "You must be bleeding barmy, the lot of you."

"Why are you taking us down there, then?" Gertie asked belligerently.

"'Cos I don't want to see you get in trouble, that's what. If Sid throws you out, you'll have to walk home. Some of the lads could be riled up enough to follow you."

"You're more worried about bleeding Doris than you are the rest of us," Gertie muttered.

Doris gasped. "Oh, Miss Brown!"

"Maybe I am," Samuel said, staring straight ahead. "But as long as she's with you, I'm sticking close to you all."

"Well, you'd better not bleeding interfere when we get down there," Gertie warned.

"I'll stay out of the way, unless there's trouble."

Ethel nudged Gertie in the ribs. "Do you think we'd better forget about it? Maybe it isn't such a good idea—"

"Blinking strewth!" Gertie glared at each of her companions in turn. "All right, we'll take a vote. Just remember that's what this is all about, being able to vote for who and what we bloody want. Now, which of you bleeding crybabies wants to forget about all this and go back to the hotel?"

The rest of them looked at each other. Ethel opened her mouth to say something, then shut it again when Gertie scowled at her. Doris and Daisy exchanged glances, but neither of them said a word.

Satisfied, Gertie sat back in her seat. "All right. That's bleeding settled, then. Now, who's going to be the one what gives them the bloody challenge?"

"You are," everyone chorused, while Doris's voice trailed after them with a faint, ". . . Miss Brown."

"Right. And when they start to argue, which one of you is going to tell them exactly why we're bleeding doing this?"

Dead silence greeted her question.

"Sounds like you are, Gertie," Samuel said cheerfully.

"Bleeding heck, I have to do every bloody thing around here." Gertie huffed out her breath. "All right, then. Since I'm the only one what knows how to bleeding talk, I'll do it. But you had all better be bloody standing there right behind me, or I promise you there'll be flipping hell to pay when we get back."

They sat in silence, each with their own thoughts, as the chestnut clopped noisily along the street. Long before they reached the pub, they could hear the muffled shouts of raised voices and raucous laughter. Gertie felt quivery inside, and assured herself that it was simply the chill night air that made her shiver.

The trap jerked to a halt several yards before they reached the door. "You'd better get down here," Samuel said, turning in his seat. "I'll turn the trap around and wait for you."

"Mercy," Ethel muttered. "What am I doing here?"

Gertie was beginning to ask herself the same question. Squaring her shoulders, she faced the door of the George and Dragon and took a deep breath. She was leading her followers into the bleeding battle and striking a bloody blow for women's rights here tonight, she reminded herself.

"Come on," she said, through teeth that were tightly clenched, "let's go and prove to them that we're as bleeding good as they are."

"But we don't know how to play darts, Miss Brown," Doris said nervously as they drew closer to the rowdy clamor behind the door of the public bar. "None of us has ever played before, except you."

"And she couldn't hit the dartboard, let alone the bull's-eye," Ethel muttered.

Daisy sighed. "We haven't got a hope of winning."

"That ain't the bleeding point, is it?" Gertie said in a fierce whisper. "It's the fact that we'll be playing darts, in the public bar, with a bunch of men. It doesn't matter who bleeding wins."

"I'd like to win," Daisy said obstinately.

"Well, we ain't bleeding going to, so there. Now, just bloody shut up and let me do the flipping talking." Gertie reached out a hand to push the door open when a shadow appeared on the other side of the stained-glass window.

She pulled her hand back just as the door swung open. A man staggered out, reeking of ale and cigar smoke. He wore a cloth cap pulled down over his eyes, and his mouth was buried beneath a tangle of bushy beard.

He paused on the step, swaying back and forth, the back of his hand raised to wipe his mouth. His eyes grew wide with astonishment as he stared at Gertie and her committee. "Well, well, well," he said in a thick mumble, "what have we bloomin' here, then?"

"We're here to see Sid Flemming," Gertie announced, "so please let us pass."

The man uttered an unpleasant laugh. "This is the public bar, ladies." He peered closer at them. "That's if you *are* ladies."

Ethel gasped, while Doris let out a nervous giggle.

Gertie drew herself up as straight as she could manage. "You wouldn't know what a bleeding lady looked like if you saw one. Now bloody stand aside. We are all going in there, so don't try to bleeding stop us."

The man shook his head and leaned closer. "Look," he muttered, "take my advice. Stay out of there tonight."

Gertie gave an impatient shake of her head. "Come on, ladies," she called out, "we're going in." She pushed past the man in the doorway, gave the door an almighty shove, and stepped inside. The rest of the group crowded in behind her, all of them pressed up so close to her she felt like a tinned sardine.

At first no one seemed to notice them. A group of men stood around the dartboard, while several more crowded in front of the long bar. Others sprawled at tables, hoisting huge tankards of beer and laughing uproariously.

Gertie squinted through the thick haze of smoke to where two men ran back and forth behind the bar. To reach Sid

Flemming, she'd have to push her way through a mob of sweaty, noisy drunks. There was no sign of Ned anywhere.

All of a sudden this venture didn't seem quite as uplifting as it had back in the comfortable confines of the Pennyfoot.

Gertie was just about to turn and get the blazes out of there when someone caught sight of the little group huddled in the doorway. He nudged his companion, who nudged someone else.

Gertie began to feel cold as one by one the men fell silent, until the noise died down completely.

A voice spoke from behind the bar. "Oh, Gawd, not again."

Someone moved through the staring crowd of men and came toward Gertie. He had a shock of red hair and eyes that reminded her of the muddy green ice that formed on Deep Willow Pond.

"What are you doing in here?" he demanded gruffly. "You don't belong in the public bar."

Gertie opened her mouth to speak, but nothing seemed to come out. She felt a sharp nudge in the small of her back as Daisy whispered fiercely, "Go on, Miss Brown, you tell them."

"We want to speak to Sid Flemming," Gertie blurted out.

"I'm Sid Flemming," the man said, leaning threateningly toward her. "So what are you going to do about it?"

Gertie tried again. "We've come to issue a challenge to the men's darts team." Her voice had sounded funny, but she'd managed to get the words out.

"We don't allow women to play darts," Sid said, scowling at them each in turn from beneath thick bushy red brows.

Gertie swallowed. "We have just as much right to—"

She got no further. First one man, then another started muttering. The muttering got louder and became jeers and catcalls. "String the bitches up by their bloody thumbs," someone called out, and a chorus of cheers greeted the words.

Someone behind her started whimpering in fright. Gertie didn't need to turn around to know that it was Ethel. Her temper rising, she sent a belligerent glance around at the jeering men, then looked back at Sid. "They don't have to get so bloody nasty about it. All we wanted was a bleeding game of darts."

"Look," Sid said, sounding almost kind in comparison to the vicious shouts of the men, "two of your lot was in here last night and just about wrecked the place. They caused a bloody riot, they did, and then one of them started chucking beer mugs against the wall. Some of the lads got hurt by flying glass, and the rest of us are a little upset about it. I think you'd all better leave before someone else gets hurt."

As if to emphasize his warning, a beer mug came flying through the air. It smashed against the wall about a foot from Gertie's shoulder and splintered into a thousand pieces.

Ethel squealed, and Gertie didn't hang around to argue. Turning tail, she lunged for the door, yelling at the top of her lungs, "Let's get the bleeding hell out of here!"

CHAPTER

❀ 19 ❀

The cold, clear air outside the pub chilled Gertie's blood. Or maybe it was the fact that some of the customers were crowding behind them, muttering ugly threats and warnings. "Come on!" she howled. "Bloody run for it!"

Her feet pounded the ground as she ran clumsily toward the trap, where Samuel sat half-turned in his seat to watch them.

"I told you," he muttered as the four of them fell into the seats. Cracking the whip, he urged the chestnut forward, sending Ethel's elbow crashing into Gertie's face.

"Ow!" she yelled, shoving Ethel into the seat beside her. "That bleeding hurt."

"You're lucky you weren't all killed," Samuel muttered as the trap bounced and lurched painfully along the road.

Gradually the shouts died away behind them, and Gertie began to relax. "Strewth," she said, mopping her forehead with her sleeve, "that was a bleeding close call."

Doris and Daisy sat huddled together on the seat opposite her, neither of them looking as if they wanted to discuss their narrow shave. Ethel's teeth were chattering, though Gertie wasn't sure if it was fright or perhaps the cold wind that caused it.

"What the dickens did you do to stir 'em up like that?" Samuel demanded as he pulled on the reins to slow down the mare. "I thought they were going to stone all of you."

"We didn't bleeding do nothing," Gertie muttered, draping her scarf over her head to keep her ears warm. "It were them bleeding suffragettes what got them all riled up, weren't it? Why didn't you tell us they bloody smashed up the place last night?"

Samuel shook his head. "I didn't know they'd done that. I wasn't down there last night. It doesn't surprise me, though. They've been causing a lot of trouble down there."

"Well, this time some of the men got bleeding hurt." Gertie shook her head. "I never thought they'd go that bleeding far. It's not right that people get bloody hurt. How can they expect people to sympathize with their flipping cause if they're going about hurting people?"

"That's the trouble with causes," Samuel said, flicking the reins gently across the chestnut's back. "Someone always gets hurt."

"I don't want to hurt no one, Miss Brown," Doris said with a tremor in her voice. "I don't think I want to be treated equal if I have to be violent about it."

"Me neither," Ethel fervently agreed. "I can't wait to get back to my Joe, even if he does tell me what to do all the time."

"I'll take you home after I drop this lot off," Samuel said, sounding disgusted with them all.

"Well, I bloody believe in the Women's Movement and what they're fighting for," Gertie said after giving it some thought. "But I think there has to be a better blinking way to go about it."

"I think we should all marry toffs," Doris declared. "Then we wouldn't have to worry about anything except how to spend the money."

Samuel grunted. "You'd have a lot more than that to worry about if you married a toff, let me tell you."

Gertie settled herself more comfortably in the seat. "Well, that's something I won't have to bleeding worry about. I'm bleeding off all men for good. That bloody Ned weren't nowhere around when all that trouble started. Fat lot of bleeding good he were. Him and all his flipping big talk. You're bloody better off without them, that's what I blinking say."

"That's how I feel," Daisy declared. "Though I wish there were some way to have babies without them."

"I'd think about that if I was you," Gertie said, her gaze on the shadowy ocean. "It ain't easy having babies without a man to help take care of them."

"Oh, cripes," Doris muttered. "I keep forgetting."

Gertie was only half listening. "Forgetting what?"

Idly she watched Doris dig in the pocket of her skirt and bring out a crumpled envelope. Then her heart skipped a beat as Doris thrust it at her, saying nervously, "Ned gave it to me this afternoon, but every time I went to give it to you, something happened."

Gertie's stomach seemed to twist up in a ball. She took the envelope from Doris and peered at it.

"What is it?" Ethel demanded, leaning closer. "Who's it from?"

"I don't bleeding know, do I," Gertie said, feeling her heart begin to pound. "I don't know who the heck would be bleeding writing to me."

"Maybe it's Ian," Ethel said, giving Gertie a nudge in the ribs. "Maybe he wants you back again."

"Well, he'll be bleeding unlucky." Gertie thrust the envelope into the pocket of her coat.

"Aren't you going to read it?" Ethel said, sounding disappointed.

"I can't, can I," Gertie said scornfully. "It's too bleeding dark. I'll have to bloody wait now until we get back home."

Not that she would have read it there in front of them, anyway, she thought, her gaze fixed on the lights of the hotel glimmering in the distance. This was something she wanted to read in private.

She had no idea who the letter was from, if it was a letter at all. She only knew who she hoped it was from. And she wouldn't know that until she was safely back inside her room in the Pennyfoot.

The idea came to Cecily when she least expected it. She had gone to visit Gertie's babies, knowing that Mrs. Chubb would be in charge of them that evening.

The twins were growing rapidly, and Cecily enjoyed the chance to spend time with them and marvel at their tiny, yet somehow miraculous accomplishments.

They were both asleep when Mrs. Chubb let her into Gertie's tiny room. Standing at the foot of the cradles, Cecily gazed down on their angelic faces. "We really must move Gertie into a bigger room, Altheda," she murmured. "These children must have room to play."

"Yes, mum. I was thinking the same thing myself. Growing faster than weeds, they are."

"So I can see." Cecily tore her gaze away from the babies and smiled at Mrs. Chubb. "It was nice of you to sit with them tonight. I hope the maids are enjoying their free evening."

"I'm sure they are, mum. Though goodness knows where they went. Kept it all a secret, they did."

"Well, I'm sure they'll tell you all about it when they return."

"I don't know about that, mum. These young girls nowadays are not like we were when we were young. Got their heads full of all this modern way of thinking, they have. All this stuff and nonsense about men and women being equal. Can't do them any good, that's what I say. Men are not going to change, no matter how much the women complain about it.''

"One can hope, Mrs. Chubb," Cecily murmured.

"If you ask me, they're going about it all wrong. I always got my own way with Fred, God rest his soul.'' Mrs. Chubb leaned over the cradle and drew the blanket over Lilly's plump shoulders. "It was just a matter of putting the ideas in his head, then making him think he'd thought of it first, that's all.''

Cecily smiled. "Is it really that simple?"

Mrs. Chubb smiled. "It really is, mum. It's amazing what you can make a man believe, if you know how to go about it the right way.''

"Or a woman for that matter,'' Cecily said softly.

The housekeeper raised her eyebrows. "Beg pardon, mum?''

Cecily patted her on the shoulder. "It's all right, Altheda, I was talking to myself. By the way, did you happen to send up a tray to Lady Katherine this evening?''

"Yes, I did, mum.'' Mrs. Chubb looked worried. "Which reminds me, the tray hasn't been brought down. I don't know what time the girls will be back. I'd better fetch it myself. Perhaps you wouldn't mind keeping an eye on the twins while I'm gone?''

"I have a better idea.'' Cecily opened the door. "I want a word with Lady Katherine, so I'll fetch the tray myself.''

"Oh, no, mum, I couldn't—''

"Don't worry about it, Altheda. It wouldn't be the first time.''

"I know, mum, but—''

Cecily held up her hand to forestall any more protests. "It's settled.'' She turned to go, then looked back at the housekeeper. "Did you happen to notice what was on the tray, by any chance?''

Mrs Chubb looked worried. "Yes, mum. It was vichyssoise and the steak-and-kidney pie.''

Cecily nodded. "And the salad?"

"Lobster, mum. Michel wanted to use the rest of them up."

"I was rather hoping he would."

Cecily was about to close the door when Mrs. Chubb said anxiously, "The lobster's all right, isn't it, mum? I mean, no one else got sick, I hope?"

"Everyone else is fine, Altheda, I promise you."

"Oh, good, mum. I just thought, what with the meeting tomorrow and all—"

Cecily shook her head. "The meeting is about something entirely different. Something a good deal more pleasant."

Mrs. Chubb sighed in relief, though her eyes still looked worried. "Very well, mum."

Cecily left her with her sleeping charges and hurried up the stairs to Lady Katherine's suite. The widow answered her knock promptly, though she appeared surprised to see Cecily standing there.

"Oh, Mrs. Sinclair! I thought it was one of the maids come to take away my tray."

"As a matter of fact, Lady Katherine, that is why I wished to see you." Cecily placed her hand on the door. "May I come in?"

The widow looked apprehensive. "Well, as a matter of fact, I was just preparing to retire for the night. I am planning to leave in the morning, you know."

"It won't take a minute," Cecily promised her.

Obviously reluctant, Lady Katherine stepped back to allow her to enter. "I do like to retire early when I have to travel," she murmured. "Especially now that I shall be traveling alone. So much more stressful, of course."

"Of course," Cecily agreed. She glanced across at the buffet, where a tray of empty dishes stood. "If you like, I can take the tray down with me. Then you won't be disturbed for the rest of the night."

"Oh, how terribly kind of you, Mrs. Sinclair." Lady Katherine seemed distracted as she wandered over to the bed. "That is most thoughtful of you, indeed."

Cecily started toward the buffet. "I do hope you enjoyed your supper?"

"Very much. Yes, thank you."

"Well, that's a relief." Cecily picked up the tray. "The lobster salad was satisfactory, I trust?"

"Excellent." Lady Katherine picked up a sequin-trimmed fan and waved it in front of her face.

"Better than the other night?" Cecily persisted.

"Much, much better. I enjoyed every bite."

"Oh, I'm so glad." Halfway across the room, Cecily paused. "As a matter of fact, Lady Katherine, I have an apology to make. You see, you were given the wrong salad tonight, and I was concerned that it might not have tasted fresh."

Lady Katherine slowly lowered her fan. "The wrong salad?"

"Yes. Earlier this afternoon a lobster salad had been sent back from a room untouched. Apparently, the maid who set up your tray tonight mistook the returned plate for a fresh one. She placed the salad on your tray and brought it up with the rest of your meal." Cecily turned and headed for the door. "I can't imagine why the salad wasn't thrown out," she murmured. "I'll have to chastise my staff for that omission. I am relieved, however, that you found the salad so enjoyable." She balanced the tray on her hip and opened the door.

"Just a moment," Lady Katherine said sharply.

Cecily looked back at her with an expression of pure innocence. "Yes?"

"Who . . . where . . ." The widow seemed to have trouble forming the words. She ran the tip of her tongue over her lips and muttered hoarsely, "Who was it who sent the salad back, Mrs. Sinclair?"

Cecily turned fully around to face her. "As a matter of fact, I do believe it came back from Miss DelRay's room."

"No!" The chilling whisper seemed to echo across the room.

Cecily walked back into the room. "Is there something the matter, Lady Katherine? If you are distressed about eating someone else's salad, I'll be happy to send up a fresh one immediately."

The widow's hand fluttered at her throat. Her face had turned quite pale, except for a high spot of color on each cheek. "No, no," she whispered. "Please, you must send for the doctor at once."

"Dr. Prestwick? I'm afraid it's after his office hours now. I'll be happy to send for him in the morning, however—"

"I cannot wait until morning," Lady Katherine cried. "You don't understand. I must see him at once. You see, I've been poisoned."

Very carefully Cecily set the tray down on a small round table. "Poisoned?"

"Yes, yes! I demand that you send for the doctor right away. Every minute is crucial."

"But I don't understand," Cecily said, drawing closer to the bed. "Why do you think you've been poisoned?"

"The lobster salad!" Tears spurted from Lady Katherine's eyes. Her hand trembled violently as she stretched it out in a beseeching gesture. "The poison was in the salad."

"Oh, I don't think so," Cecily said soothingly. "I ate some myself for lunch and I am perfectly fine. I would say that you are merely suffering from a tummy upset. Lobster will do that sometimes, you know. Though I can understand why you are frightened, after what happened to your husband—"

Lady Katherine suddenly lunged at Cecily and grasped her blouse with both hands. "For God's sake, you stupid woman, I am dying!"

"Now, now." Cecily dislodged the clawing fingers and moved back. "I'm quite sure a good night's sleep will do wonders. If you are not better in the morning, I'll send for the doctor—''

''I will be dead by the morning!'' Lady Katherine threw aside the bedcovers and came up on her hands and knees. Her eyes narrowed like those of a spitting cat. ''Listen to me, you nattering nitwit. I have been poisoned. I should know what I'm talking about. I put the poison in the salad myself. If you do not send for the doctor this very minute, I will end up just like Bertram, and my death will be on your conscience.''

''Did you also put the poison in your husband's salad?'' Cecily asked innocently.

Rearing straight up on her knees, her hands flailing the air, Lady Katherine yelled, ''Yes, I did! He deserved to die. He and that dirty slut down the hall with whom he was carrying on. Now get that damn doctor at once.''

''I have one more question first,'' Cecily said calmly.

The widow's voice rose to a scream. ''What? What?''

''How did my gardener die?''

All of a sudden Lady Katherine seemed to deflate like a spoiled soufflé. She sank onto her heels and covered her eyes with her hands. ''He saw me picking the blossoms,'' she said, her voice low and hoarse from screaming. ''He tried to stop me. I shoved him away, and he fell. He said he was going to tell the constable . . . I couldn't let him.''

She lowered her hands and in a childish voice added, ''I couldn't, could I? I had to keep him quiet. The shears were on the ground. I picked them up and stabbed him with them.'' She shook her head as if to clear it. ''There was so much blood. All over my gown. I had to rush back to the hotel before anyone saw me. That old fool of a colonel spied me from his window. I heard him shout, but I don't think he recognized me.''

Cecily briefly closed her eyes. So John had been deliberately murdered after all. She could not feel at all sorry for this woman, who would most certainly hang for her heinous crimes.

"I will send for Dr. Prestwick," she said as calmly as her anger would allow. "I would suggest that you lie as still as possible until he arrives. That way the poison won't travel through your system quite as fast."

Lady Katherine obediently lay flat on her back. "Hurry," she whispered, closing her eyes. "Please . . . hurry."

Cecily left her there to deal with her terror. She quietly stepped out into the hallway and closed the door behind her, satisfied that Lady Katherine would not move again until the constable arrived.

The sudden movement at her side startled her for a moment. "There you are, Baxter. You heard everything, I take it?"

"Indeed I did." He spoke quietly, drawing her further along the hallway before adding, "I have to admit, your plan was a brilliant one. As always. I am very proud of you, my dear madam. You are an intelligent woman."

His features were softened by the glow of the gas lamps as she looked up at him. It made him look almost vulnerable. She couldn't help teasing him a little. "Are you inferring that I'm unique? There are many intelligent women in this world."

"Ah, but I am interested in only one of them."

Completely disarmed, she murmured, "Thank you, Baxter." Heading for the stairs, she added, "I'm just happy that the plan worked out so well."

"How ironic that Lady Katherine should believe she was poisoned by her own hand," Baxter said, pausing at the top of the stairs to allow Cecily to descend first.

"Poor Lady Katherine. I can't help feeling just a little bit sorry for her. She is in for a very bad night, I'm afraid. Although she is in the best of health, of course. I'm quite sure she will be furious when she discovers that I invented the entire story in the hopes that she would be frightened into confessing what she had done." Reaching the landing on the floor of her suite, she waited for Baxter to join her.

"I'll send Samuel to fetch P. C. Northcott first thing in the morning," he said as they walked down the hallway together. "This is one of those times when a telephone would be of great value."

"I agree. I'm quite excited about implementing some of our plans for the hotel. I plan to mention a few of them at the staff meeting tomorrow if you approve."

"Of course. I must confess I'm rather looking forward to being presented as the new part owner of the Pennyfoot Hotel."

She smiled up at him. "I know everyone will be as pleased with the new arrangement as I am."

"I hope so." He paused long enough to draw her to him and kiss her on the cheek. "Until the morning, my dear madam."

"Sleep well, Baxter."

"I think I shall now."

He left her, and she entered her suite, closing the door behind her. She was also looking forward to the meeting tomorrow. She only hoped that the staff wouldn't be concerned by the news that Baxter now owned half of the Pennyfoot.

She must remember to reassure them that there would be no significant changes, and they would not lose their jobs. In fact, if some of Baxter's ideas were implemented, everyone would be in for some pleasant surprises.

CHAPTER

✿ 20 ✿

"I hope you all had a good time tonight," Mrs. Chubb said as Gertie bent down to plop a kiss on James's head. "Though I must say, you weren't gone long."

"Ah, we just went for a walk along the Esplanade, that's all." Gertie straightened and smiled at the housekeeper. "Thanks, Mrs. Chubb. I really am grateful for you taking care of the nippers for me."

Mrs. Chubb shook her head. "No need to thank me. It's a pleasure to watch them. I don't see very much of them, and after all, they are my surrogate grandchildren. They'll be all grown up before you can turn around."

Gertie dragged off her coat and hung it on the hook behind the door. She could almost feel the letter burning in the pocket. Anxious now to be rid of the housekeeper so that she could find out who had written to her, she opened her mouth in a huge yawn. "I can't wait for them to grow up. Then they can bleeding take care of themselves.''

Mrs. Chubb looked shocked. ''You don't mean that, Gertie Brown. The greatest joy a woman can have is watching her children grow up. All too soon they'll be off on lives of their own. Look at poor Madam. She never sees her sons, and now she has a grandson she'll never see neither. It isn't right, that's what I say.''

''Madam's a bleeding grandmother? When did that bloody happen, then?''

''Never you mind,'' Mrs. Chubb said sharply. ''And don't go spreading the news all around the hotel. Madam will tell us when she wants us to know. In fact, I wouldn't be surprised if that's why she's called a staff meeting for tomorrow morning.''

''Flipping strewth, I'd bleeding forgotten about that.'' Gertie opened her mouth in another monstrous yawn. ''I s'pose I'd better get to bed if I have to get up bleeding earlier in the morning. I've got a lot to do before I can go to any flipping meeting.''

''Just make sure you're there,'' Mrs. Chubb said, finally taking the hint. ''I promised Madam we'd all be there.''

Gertie watched the door close behind the bulky hips of Mrs. Chubb and breathed a sigh of relief. At last she was alone. Now she could finally read her letter.

Drawing the oil lamp closer, she turned it up as high as it could go. Then she took the letter out of her coat pocket and carried it back to the bed. Settling herself down, she looked at the envelope. The postmark was smudged and impossible to read in the dim, flickering light from the lamp.

Now that the time had finally come, she was reluctant to open it. She'd only ever had one letter in her life before, and that was from her father. She knew her father's handwriting. It looked like a spider with muddy feet had crawled across the bleeding page.

This writing was quite different, her name penned with

a flourish in big bold letters. *Gertie Brown*. "Please," she whispered aloud, "please don't let it be Ian."

She stared at the writing for a long time, then took a shaky breath. Very carefully she slipped her thumb under the flap and tore it open.

Her fingers shook so much as she unfolded the page, she had to lay the letter down on the table. She smoothed it out, pushing it closer to the oil lamp so that she could read it properly.

She read the signature at the bottom of the page first, and caught her breath. In beautiful scroll, the name seemed to leap from the page. Ross McBride.

Slowly she began to read, savoring each word.

My dear Gertie, I have waited a long time to write to you. So many times I sat down to write, but then I told myself you wouldn't want to hear from an old man like me. I tried very hard to forget you, lass, but I can't seem to stop thinking about you. I keep remembering the kiss we shared in the card room, and the last time I saw you, sitting next to me in the conservatory while you told me you couldn't marry me.

Gertie blinked hard, brushed a tear from her eye, and went on reading. Ross wrote about his daily life, his work on the railroad, and the people he knew in the village where he lived. The way he described it, the village sounded very much like Badgers End, except there were mountains to look at instead of the ocean.

She turned the page, eagerly scanning the lines. All too soon, she came to the last paragraph.

I can't forget you, Gertie, no matter how hard I try. I think about you all the time, and I have never stopped wanting you and your wee bairns here beside me. I know I rushed you before, lass, and I'm sorry for that. It wasn't fair of me. I know that. I won't pester you again, I promise. I just want to write to you and hear from you now and then. Tell me how the bairns are. They must be starting

*to walk soon. I'll understand, lass, if you'd rather not write.
I just had to try one more time. Yours everlasting, Ross*

Gertie read the letter again. She laid it down on the table
and got up to look at her babies still sleeping soundly in
their cradles. She looked down on them for a long time.
Then she went back to the table, opened the drawer, and
pulled out the sheets of hotel stationery and the pen she
used to write instructions for Daisy.

Carefully she unscrewed the top of the ink bottle, then
dipped the nib of the pen into the ink. She shook off a drop
or two into the bottle, then slowly and laboriously she began to write. *Dear Ross* . . .

P. C. Northcott arrived early the next morning. Cecily was
faced with the unenviable task of informing Lady Katherine
that she was about to be arrested for the murder of her
husband and John Thimble.

She finally managed to convince the widow that she was
not about to die, at least not from the poison, and then left
her to get dressed. P. C. Northcott had then taken Lady
Katherine to Wellercombe in the police carriage, where she
would be formally charged with murder.

Now that the situation had been resolved, Cecily could
concentrate on the meeting with her staff. Once more in
her suite, the sun streamed through her window as she rehearsed the words she wanted to say. She was glad that
Baxter would be there by her side.

She would have to see about hiring a new gardener, she
thought, eyeing the dew-covered lawns. The grounds would
quickly become unkempt if neglected for too long.

She had promised to meet Baxter in the roof garden before the meeting, as he had some ideas he wanted to discuss
with her about the new design.

He was waiting for her as usual, looking most suave and
debonair in his black morning coat and gray pin-striped
trousers. The sky had clouded considerably since she'd

risen that morning, and judging by the dark mass hovering over the sea, rain was imminent. A gust of wind dislodged several strands of her hair, and she captured them with her hand as she smiled at Baxter.

"I think that autumn is upon us," he observed, his gaze settling on her face.

"I believe you are right." She walked past him and stood in front of the wall that overlooked the rose garden. "I don't suppose we shall have too many more opportunities to stand here like this until the spring."

He didn't answer her right away, and she turned to look at him, disturbed by the odd expression on his face. "Is something wrong?" she asked quickly.

"No, nothing." He smiled, and as always she was fascinated by the changes it brought to his face. "I was just thinking how fortunate I am to be here with you."

"You might have a change of heart," she warned him, only half jesting. "I have become quite set in my ways since James passed away. I might find it difficult to adjust to a partner at first."

His smile faded. "I wouldn't ask you to change your ways, Cecily."

"I'm assured of that. It's just . . ."

His frown deepened. "What is it, Cecily? If you have had second thoughts about our partnership, then admit it to me now. I have no wish to force you into a situation that would make you unhappy."

She quickly placed a hand on his arm. "Oh, Bax, of course I haven't any second thoughts. It is just that sometimes I think our difference in attitudes could prove to be a problem between us."

"How so? Tell me, and I will do my best to understand."

She looked up at him. "I have been free to make my own decisions for a long time now. I'm not used to consulting with someone else. I am a little afraid that we might clash at times."

"I am fully aware of that."

She nodded. "I thought you might be."

"Cecily, a difference of opinion now and again is not going to destroy what we have. I have no intention of dictating to you how to live your personal life. Our mutual decisions will be based on what is best for the hotel and its staff. Other than that, you are quite free to go your own way. Within reason, of course."

She was glad he'd added the last sentence. For a moment she'd thought he was displaying a little too much indifference. Nevertheless, she sought reassurance.

"Within what reason?' she asked lightly.

He raised an eyebrow at her. "I think you know quite well. The reason I came back to the Pennyfoot, the reason I left in the first place, was because I care for you a great deal. I know it is far too soon to place any impositions upon you. We have only just begun this courtship. I do hope, however, that you will bear in mind that my intentions are honorable."

"Of course, Baxter. I have always known that."

"Particularly in the case of Dr. Prestwick."

She would have laughed had he not looked so serious. "I can assure you, Baxter," she said gravely, "I have no personal interest whatsoever in Kevin Prestwick. As a matter of fact, he has become quite distant ever since he discovered that you had returned to Badgers End. I think he suspects that our new relationship is not solely a business one."

"Hm." Baxter placed his hands behind his back and rocked back and forth on his heels. "The man has more perception than I'd supposed."

In spite of the terse comment, Cecily could tell he was well pleased. Deciding it was time to change the subject, she took a long look around the garden.

The honeysuckle blossoms had long since faded from the trellis, though a few of the roses planted in the huge wooden barrels still glowed a dark red. "I am looking forward to rearranging this garden. We really must find a new gardener before too long.''

''I shall see about it immediately. What do you think about placing a large ornamental birdbath in the corner over there?''

''I'd love it. Do you think we should keep the trellis? Wisteria would be nice, don't you think?''

She spent the next ten minutes happily discussing the renovations, content just to be alone in his company.

''I think it's time we went down to the ballroom,'' Baxter said at last, pulling his pocket watch from his vest pocket.

''Then let us go.'' She linked her arm through his. ''I'm anxious to present the new part owner of the Pennyfoot Hotel.''

''I'll do my best to make you happy, Cecily.''

She smiled up at him. ''You already have, Baxter. More than you will ever know.''